Jessica didn't know what she'd find

Pausing only long enough to pay the taxi driver, she sprinted into the building in an upper-middle-class section of Washington, D.C.

She'd caught the last flight out of Ohio shortly after midnight when Suzette repeatedly failed to answer her phone. Now past 2:00 a.m., Jessica's heart raced as she neared her friend's door. The key wasn't necessary; at a slight nudge, the door swung open.

For a moment, Jessica blinked, barely able to believe her eyes. A scream was welling up in her throat even before she heard the door click shut behind her. She turned in the direction of the sound, but before she could, something dark and heavy was pulled down over her eyes and mouth. Cold metal jabbed mercilessly into her throat, and then miraculously, unexpectedly, there was nothing but a black void.

ABOUT THE AUTHOR

Cathy Gillen Thacker is a full-time novelist who once taught piano to children. Born and raised in Ohio, she attended Miami University. After moving cross-country several times, she now resides in Texas with her husband and three children. A prolific writer, she has penned twelve Harlequin American Romances and two Harlequin Temptations.

Books by Cathy Gillen Thacker

Dream Spinners

Cathy Gillen Thacker

Harlequin Books

TORONTO • NEW YORK • LONDON
AMSTERDAM • PARIS • SYDNEY • HAMBURG
STOCKHOLM • ATHENS • TOKYO • MILAN

Harlequin Intrigue edition published December 1988

ISBN 0-373-22104-5

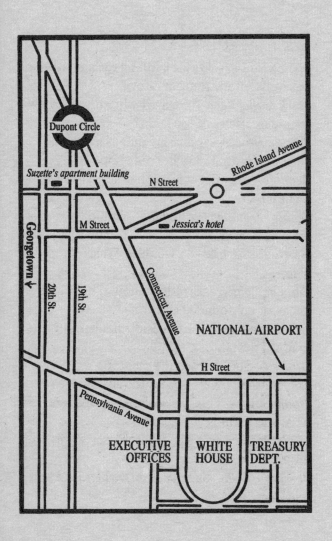

CAST OF CHARACTERS

Jessica Lowell—Was she falling for a man who was only out for a steamy story?

Mark Gallagher—An expert with the lens, how was he in affairs of the heart?

Suzette Howar—A missing manuscript and personal journal were her only hope.

Bennett Agee—How far would he go to save the senator?

Senator Douglas Rothschild—Would he *kill* for the presidency?

Gloria Rothschild—A troubled Washington wife.

Pamela Fieldler—Erratic, cunning, her bizarre behavior confounded everyone.

Dr. Ethan Conti—His bedside manner put him in much demand.

Audrey—She guarded the senator's unblemished reputation...too zealously?

Noah Chase—This CIA chief knew instinctively what was coming.

Craig Rothschild—The senator's son always ran afoul of the law.

Tamara North—Suzette's elusive literary agent had much to hide.

Chapter One

"Jessica, you've got to help me—"

Jessica smiled at Suzette's breathless tone. For her old college roommate, everything was an emergency. "Anything for a friend, Suzette. You know that."

"Put me up for a few weeks?"

Jessica paused at the unexpected anxiety in Suzette's voice. "What about the plans we had to get together next month?" They'd spent days planning what they would do when they got together again during their regularly scheduled vacations. And Suzette knew Jessica had little leeway in her job as a staff writer and reporter for the *Spring Valley Sentinel*. If she came now, Jessica wouldn't be able to see her as much, because she'd still have to work.

"Forget our plans, Jessica. I've got to get away now—tonight, before it's too late."

Too late for what? Jessica wondered. Aware of her friend Bennett Agee lingering in the background—it was seven o'clock and they'd just come back from dinner—Jessica turned away from him. Whatever was going on with Suzette was private, as was Jessica's counsel to her. "What's the problem?" Jessica asked tensely in a low tone. Suzette had always been dramatic, flamboyant.

But never before had she confessed to being scared, or even hinted she might be in some sort of jeopardy. "Has something happened at work or in your personal life?"

For a moment it seemed Suzette wouldn't answer. Finally she said in a low voice that shook slightly, "You know that project I've been working on? Well, it's been going almost *too well*. I've finally got some answers and I'm scared, Jessica. Really scared." An edge crept into her voice, and she spoke even more rapidly than before. "Please, Jessica, just put me up for a few weeks. I need someplace safe to stay, someplace quiet where I can think. I also need to finish my novel. I only have a couple chapters left to write."

"How's...?" Jessica almost said "Dreams of Glory," then remembering Bennett's presence, censored herself and said, "Uh...your work on that going?"

"My agent is very excited about it, at least what she's read so far, the first three hundred pages."

"That's wonderful! Are you going to let me read it?"

"You'll be the first one, once it's completed." Suzette paused. "I really need your opinion on what I've done."

"Great, so when can I expect you?" she asked briskly.

"Ten. I'm booked on the last flight on Northeast Airlines out of National Airport."

"Did you rent a car?"

"No. Not this time." There was a tense silence that reeked of fear. "Would you mind terribly driving in to Dayton to pick me up?"

She did sound jittery, Jessica thought. Maybe too jittery to drive. "No problem," she said, forcibly injecting lightness into her tone. Whatever was going on, they would deal with it together, when Suzette arrived.

"Good." Suzette sighed. "And Jessica, don't tell anyone I'm coming."

That wouldn't be so easy to adhere to. "Bennett's here." From his vantage point in the kitchen, he could hear everything she said.

Suzette swore vituperatively, reminding Jessica anew of how much the two disliked one another. "All right, but no one else! Promise!"

"I promise."

The receiver clicked.

Bennett approached. "Trouble?"

Jessica avoided what she couldn't answer truthfully. "Suzette's taking a few days off."

His eyes narrowed in concern. "That's rather sudden, isn't it?"

Jessica shrugged, not sure why she felt the need to cover for Suzette; she trusted Bennett, they'd been friends since their elementary school days. Was it Suzette's secrecy, the tension in her voice? Or just that Suzette and Bennett had never really liked one another, despite the fact both were closely connected with Senator Rothschild's operations. Both had worked as summer interns for the senator while they were in college. Both had served as volunteers on the senator's last campaign. And now, four years later, Bennett was a salaried member of the senator's staff. A small-town lawyer with his own practice in Spring Valley, he currently ran the senator's Ohio office headquarters—commuting to DC several times a month to inform the senator about constituents' concerns. He also organized and attended the senator's monthly public appearances in his home state. Suzette, with her dual degrees in political science and journalism, served as a research assistant on the senator's staff. Very much in tune with his political views, she had written some of his better speeches. Both Bennett and Suzette had similarly ambitious natures that had entrapped them in a work-related rivalry Jessica didn't envy. Aware Bennett was still waiting for her answer, Jessica said with evasive finality, "She just needed to get away."

"She's driving in from the airport?" Bennett asked curiously.

"No. I'm picking her up."

Again his face registered surprise. He knew that Suzette, who was extraordinarily independent, liked to have a car at her disposal at all times. "When?"

"Later tonight."

Bennett ran a hand through his immaculately combed white-blond hair. His normally pale skin took on a faint pink flush as he picked up the suit coat he'd been wearing when they returned from dinner. "I'll go with you."

Under other circumstances Jessica would have welcomed his company. But not this time. "No, I think I'd better go alone." She appreciated his offer but just couldn't accept. She looked at him in a way that let him know their casual evening together was at an end. "It's one of those woman-to-woman things."

His gray eyes bore into her, searching out every veiled emotion. "You're sure?"

"Positive." Jessica swallowed hard. "And Bennett, don't mention this to anyone else."

"Why not?"

"Because I think she wants to lie low for a few days."

He shrugged, as if Suzette's plans didn't matter to him in the least. "Who would I tell?"

WAS SHE CRAZY to fly to Washington in the middle of the night? Jessica wondered as the taxi sped away from the National Airport terminal in the direction of Suzette's apartment off Connecticut Avenue, within easy reach of the Capitol. She knew Bennett would say she was. But he hadn't talked to Suzette on the phone, he hadn't heard the suppressed fear in her friend's voice. He didn't know what dangerous information Suzette had apparently uncovered. All in the name of blockbuster fiction.

But what was happening now wasn't fiction, Jessica thought, pulling her coat tighter around her against the chill of the bleak January night.

What was happening now was real. Suzette was on the run, scared out of her mind. Yet she hadn't caught her eight-thirty flight to Dayton, hadn't taken any of the others after that—at least as far as Jessica or the airlines had been able to discover. Nor was she answering her phone. When Jessica, in a panic, had tried calling her at home at eleven, all she'd gotten was a busy signal. Determined to reach Suzette and find out what was going on, Jessica had then told the operator it was an emergency and instructed her to cut in on the line. The results were worrisome. The operator had found that the receiver was apparently off the hook, and a television set was on in the background.

As far as Jessica was concerned, that had done it. She'd caught the last flight out shortly after midnight and landed at National an hour later. Now, nearing two in the morning, she was almost at Suzette's place.

The problem was, she didn't know what she would find.

Pausing only long enough to pay the taxi driver, Jessica sprinted into the building. Though in an upper-middle-class neighborhood, the building had no doorman. Anyone could walk into the carpeted halls, past the mailboxes, up the stairs....

Jessica's heart was pounding as she neared Suzette's door. She reached into her purse and took out the key Suzette had given her several years ago, when she first moved to DC. Jessica had used it only three times on prior visits to her friend. Now she could barely manage the lock, her hands were shaking so. But it turned out the key wasn't necessary. At a slight nudge, the door swung open.

For a moment Jessica blinked, barely able to believe what she saw. The apartment was a wreck. Books, papers lay scattered all over the floor. And in the midst of all that chaos, in the middle of the living-room floor lay Suzette, her mouth slack and open, her skin a peculiar pasty white.

Dimly aware of the low murmur of the television set in the background, Jessica started toward her friend. A scream was welling up in her throat even before she heard the door shut behind her.

Jessica turned in the direction of the sound. Just then something dark and heavy was pulled down over her eyes and mouth, choking and blinding her. Strong arms closed around her, further cutting off her breath. In a panic, Jessica began to struggle furiously, kicking out behind her—again to no avail. There was the sound of a man's furious muttering as he brutally intensified his grip on her. Angry now as well as scared, she kicked out again, the heel of her suede boots contacting with someone's shin. Then she felt it: a swift rapier-sharp prick in her neck. Piercing and unbearably sharp, the cold metal jabbed mercilessly into her throat, and then miraculously, unexpectedly there was only nothingness...soundless, terror-filled nothingness as she slipped into an endless black void.

"THANK GOD she's waking up!" Bennett Agee exclaimed with relief.

"She's going to be fine," the other man reassured him.

Jessica slowly opened her eyes. After blinking several times, she was able to focus on the people around her bed. Bennett was there. So was his boss, United States Senator Douglas Rothschild. Looking about her, she saw they were in an austere hospital room. It seemed like a white-walled prison. *Funny, though,* she thought groggily, she couldn't remember how she got there, when or why. Had she been in an accident? "Where am I?" she asked in a scratchy voice, her throat feeling as if it had the consistency of sandpaper.

Bennett wordlessly poured her a glass of water, and after helping her to sit up, assisted her as she took some easy sips through a straw. "You're in Potomac General."

Potomac General? Agitated, Jessica tried to sit up all the way, but couldn't. She was still too woozy.

Bennett guided her gently back against the pillows. "Jessica, take it easy. You've had a very tough time of it."

"What happened?"

"You were assaulted."

The knot in her stomach intensified. She stared at them, shocked, incredulous. This was a nightmare and she couldn't wake up. Bennett and the senator exchanged a look. "You don't remember?" Bennett looked back at Jessica.

Slowly she gave her head a painful shake. Her mind was a blank. The lack of memory frightened her. "How'd I—how'd I get to Washington?" Jessica asked, still feeling groggy and disoriented.

"You caught a plane. Suzette was supposed to visit. When she didn't show up—"

Without warning it all came back to Jessica. The flight to DC, her arrival, Suzette's apartment. "She's—" *Oh no, not Suzette, never Suzette . . .*

"Yes, she's dead. I'm sorry, Jessica. So sorry." Bennett's hand tightened its grip on her shoulder. "That it had to end like that, that you had to be the one to find her."

Jessica glanced up at him, seeing only compassion on his face. "Then it's true—?" Fuzzily she remembered walking in on the ransacked apartment.

"You were apparently assaulted soon after arriving." Bennett continued in a low, soothing tone. "The maid found you unconscious at six this morning when she went in to clean. She called the police. They called an ambulance and brought you in here for treatment."

Jessica looked at the senator. Although he barely knew her, he, too, looked very concerned. But then that wasn't surprising; he had the reputation of being avuncular. And she knew firsthand from both Bennett and Suzette that he took a very personal interest in the members of his staff. "I don't remember that," Jessica said slowly, frustrated. "Not any of it."

"Maybe it's just as well," the senator said. A handsome man in his early forties, he had jet-black hair and vivid green eyes. His aristocratic features bore testimony to the blue blood of his lineage. He had a way of making a person feel immediately at ease, of giving the impression that his philanthropic feelings were more than skin-deep. Jessica had voted for him twice, and, at Bennett's urging, had even passed out leaflets for his last campaign. She also knew both Bennett and Suzette had come to idolize him in the years they'd spent working for him. And that many political analysts thought he might very well be the next president of the United States.

The senator frowned again, focusing on Jessica as he continued telling her why her lack of memory was a blessing in disguise. "Finding your friend dead, then being assaulted . . . it had to have been a very horrifying experience."

Maybe so, but . . .

Without warning, Jessica recalled the struggle in the apartment, the hood being pulled down over her head, Suzette dead. The tears she'd been suppressing slid down her face. She brushed them away with the back of her hand. "Have they caught the person who did it?" she managed finally in a strangled tone.

Again the senator and Bennett exchanged worried glances.

"What do you mean?" Bennett asked gently.

Jessica blinked at him in amazement. Surely they knew about this, or had guessed. "The—the burglar?"

Bennett stared at her uncomprehendingly. His face whitened even more. "Jessica, regardless of what happened to you, no one murdered Suzette. Her death was a suicide."

Chapter Two

"Suicide!" Jessica sat up with a start, her grogginess fading fast. "It couldn't have been! I was there. I saw—"

"What did you see, Jessica?" the senator interrupted, his face reddening for some reason.

A chill went down her spine and Jessica paused, suddenly afraid to tell them what she knew—afraid she too would be murdered. That whoever had attacked and killed Suzette would come after Jessica again.

"Why are you so sure it wasn't suicide?" Bennett demanded tensely, moving closer to the bed.

Suddenly Jessica knew she had to tell the truth. She had to go to the authorities or risk having it happen again. She took a deep bolstering breath and looked straight at Bennett. "Her apartment had been ransacked."

There was a moment of shocked silence as Bennett and the senator exchanged concerned looks. "Wait a minute. There was no evidence of that in the police report!" the senator growled abruptly. He looked as furious, confused and frustrated as Jessica felt. He stood up straight, a tower of outrage. "They said the apartment was in normal condition. The maid substantiated that.''

"It was," Bennett interrupted impatiently.

"How do you know?" Jessica asked, feeling her palms grow moist.

"Because I was there," Bennett responded evenly, his eyes and manner steady as he looked at her frankly. "I went there a few hours ago."

Jessica was confused. She glanced at the clock on the nightstand: three o'clock; it was midafternoon. She supposed that if she'd been found at six in the morning, that had given these men time to act by now.

"Because she worked for me, the police notified me first," the senator supplied. "She had a security card on her. I then called Bennett, who took the first flight out to DC this morning."

"From the airport I went straight to police headquarters. It's a hell of a mess," Bennett continued pragmatically, putting his hands into the pockets of his Brooks Brothers suit. He compressed his lips briefly and his eyes filled with sorrow. Softening his voice, he gently informed Jessica, "I talked to the coroner. Apparently she died as the result of taking a speedball—a powerful mixture of cocaine and heroin."

"I don't believe that!" Jessica fumed as her lower lip trembled emotionally. "Suzette didn't take drugs! She was too smart for that! She never even experimented in college."

"I understand how you feel," the senator broke in gently, stepping slightly closer to the foot of the hospital bed. "I can't believe it, either. But the fact remains that she had cocaine and heroin in her system. There was a syringe with her fingerprints on it lying next to the body."

"Then someone else injected her with those drugs!"

"Who, why?" Bennett asked, baffled. It was clear from his expression he would've liked to believe that true, too.

The senator turned to Jessica. In a weary tone, he admitted to the same line of thinking. "I at first suspected murder, as well—the thought of Suzette doing drugs is just too inconceivable." He sighed heavily and thrust his hands into the pockets of his immaculately tailored suit. "But the coroner says it's just not possible. He said there were no signs of a struggle on her part, no bruises. And that the angle of the needle mark supports the theory that it was a self-inflicted dosage."

Desperate to defend her friend, having little else to go on, Jessica blurted out a response before she could think. "Suzette was afraid for her life when she called me the night she died. Did you know that?"

Bennett and the senator were both motionless. "How do you know that?" the senator asked, his eyes hard and merciless behind the horn-rimmed glasses.

"Because...because she was, that's all," Jessica said sullenly, aware that in her woozy vulnerable state she had said too much and made them suspicious. Not just of Suzette, but of herself.

Bennett was the first to discount Suzette's claim to be in danger. "Jessica, listen to me. I know you loved Suzette. I know the two of you were like sisters, and that you want to do everything to defend her memory. Believe me, the senator and I are going to try and do that, too. We've already spoken to the rest of the staff and instructed them not to make any comments to the press about Suzette or her life. We've hired a public relations firm to put together a positive portrait of Suzette for the press, so we can counteract the impression this mess has made, but—"

"Dammit, she didn't experiment with drugs!" If she had been, Jessica would have known. "*She* didn't do this to herself."

"Then who did?" Bennett demanded impatiently. A lawyer, he wanted irrefutable evidence to back up her claim, at the very least a hint as to who might be responsible. But unfortunately Jessica didn't know.

"Look, I know you're tired," Bennett began again in a soothing voice.

Angry tears flooded Jessica's eyes, blurring her vision, but she kept her chin up. "You're right. I feel like hell."

"I also know you were one of the last people to talk to Suzette—"

Jessica felt an immediate cloak of guilt fall around her. "And when I did, she told me she was in danger!" If only she had been able to do more for her friend, if she'd gotten to Washington faster...

"Maybe we should go back to Suzette's apartment, have a look around," Senator Rothschild suggested grimly. Clearly worried, he looked at Bennett. "If Jessica's right, we owe it to Suzette to find out what really happened." His voice dropped another notch, turning husky and roughly emotional, as if he were blaming himself, too. "We owe it to ourselves."

Jessica shared the senator's bewilderment, frustration and sense of futility. Grief was there as well, lurking in the corners of her heart, but right now she refused to give in to it or express it.

She fought hospital resistance and half an hour later, with the senator's help, she'd finally arranged her release, signing herself out against the advice of the physician. Jessica knew she should be resting, but also realized she wouldn't be able to do so with all these questions floating around in her head. Besides, she wanted to concentrate on her anger, to let her rage give her strength. Finding out what had really happened to Suzette in those last few hours after they had spoken on the phone was the least she could do for her friend.

As soon as the men left to get the limo, Jessica, still feeling a bit shaky, got dressed in the same woolen sweater and slacks she'd been wearing when she arrived in Washington. Her hands trembled with reaction and fatigue as she twisted her long blond hair into a clumsy chignon at the nape of her neck. Surveying her reflection, Jessica frowned. While the turquoise blue of her sweater brought out the blue in her eyes, and the well-tailored lines of her coordinated outfit made the most of her tall slim frame and almost too-slender curves, she still looked shell-shocked, and there were violet-blue shadows beneath her eyes that would be days going away. She also felt unbearably shaky, and that showed in the faint trembling of her lips. Irritated by her continued weakness, Jessica went out to join the two men.

Half an hour later they arrived at the apartment house where Suzette had lived. This time Jessica had to use her key to get inside. When she swept in, she was amazed. The apartment was immaculate. Incredibly immaculate.

Bennett looked around, apparently seeing nothing amiss. "You see, the place was not ransacked."

All Jessica saw was that someone had gone to great lengths to cover up what had really happened that night. After all, several hours had lapsed between when she'd stumbled through the door and the time the maid found her in the morning. But realizing from the perplexed look on Bennett's face that he really didn't know what she'd seen, she said nothing in response to his assessment that everything was as before, under the circumstances, anyway.

"Now what's wrong?" he asked irritably, watching as her reporter's mind worked at full speed.

"It's too neat," Jessica said as she walked around the room. Suzette had been the consummate slob. Even if the apartment hadn't been ransacked, it never would've looked that good, especially right before her twice-monthly maid was due to come.

"Maybe you just imagined the place was ransacked," Bennett said. "After all, you were tired from the flight and the hours of worry. Then to come in and find her—maybe everything seemed a little out of focus, in the twilight zone to you."

Could she have dreamed it? Hallucinated?

All Jessica had to do was close her eyes and she would remember the sight of her friend. *Dead. No.* That was real. As was the fact that someone had been there—an intruder Jessica had never got a good look at. Someone who had tried not to kill her, but to drug her, too. Or maybe the intruder had drugged Jessica intending to kill her, but somehow she had beaten him and survived. Certainly that would explain why Jessica remembered nothing from the time she arrived at the apartment until she awakened in the hospital. Why the ambulance attendants thought she had totally flipped out or had an emotional collapse. The problem lay in getting anyone to believe her, when she had no proof.

Maybe it was best just to be quiet, at least for now. Maybe she would be safer that way. And maybe, just maybe, if she did keep quiet, the murderer would reveal him—or her—self to her.

Bennett was beside her again, gently touching her arm. "I'm sorry if I seem callous to you. I'm not. I am sorry Suzette is dead. But I can't overturn the coroner's report without disregarding the evidence. In the meantime, I have to think about how the revelation of how she died is going to affect the senator and everyone else around him."

Senator Rothschild was in the kitchen, looking around carefully. He didn't hear what Bennett said.

"You never did like her," Jessica accused him, feeling herself beginning to get emotional again.

"We didn't have anything in common," Bennett said, inspecting the neatly ordered bookshelves on either side of the entertainment center that housed the television set and stereo. "But even if we had, you must admit, Jess, Suzette wasn't the most easily decipherable person."

Jessica sighed, remembering. They had never gotten along, Bennett and Suzette. Bennett hadn't been able to see what she saw in Suzette, and vice versa. From the first they'd been involved in some kind of bizarre rivalry over Jessica's affections. Bennett felt he had first rights because he'd known her since they were young, both of them growing up fatherless in the same small Ohio town, whereas Suzette hadn't met Jessica until they roomed together at Miami University. Yet their mutual love of the written word had created a powerful bond.

Setting aside all argument, Jessica began to search.

To her relief—she wasn't sure how she would've explained Suzette's secret writing project at that point—she didn't stumble across any manuscript pages, or her private journal. She wasn't surprised. Suzette never would've left such private material out for just anyone to read. But she was a little puzzled as to where Suzette *would* have hidden them, and she determined to search again when alone and locate them.

In the meantime, to their mutual frustration, no one found anything at all out of place. There was no evidence of any drugs in the apartment. Suzette's many books on the Washington scene—everything from biographies to fiction to tour guides—were all neatly shelved next to her books on the fundamentals of writing. Her portable electric typewriter was in a case beside her desk. The papers lying there were mostly bills. Jessica remembered from her brief conversation with Bennett on the ride over here that the police had been unable to find any drugs or related paraphernalia in the two-bedroom apartment, nor any significant correspondence. Though Jessica felt encouraged about the drug report, she was less so about the lack of correspondence.

She could also see that the senator and Bennett weren't as impressed by the good news. In fact, the more she looked at them, the more she knew they were both holding something back. "You know something, don't you?" she finally asked Bennett as they reassembled in the living room, having scoured the place. When he didn't answer, she looked at the senator. "Something you haven't told me?"

Finally the senator nodded. "Suzette was having some...problems. I don't know anything about them, except she'd been seeing a psychiatrist the past couple of months. Dr. Ethan Conti. She told me once, when I asked her how she was doing, that it helped."

"Suzette—seeing a shrink?" Jessica was incredulous. She didn't believe any of it. Suzette hadn't killed herself. She hadn't been seeing a psychiatrist. She hadn't been unstable, living on the edge. None of it . . . none of it could be true.

THE PROBLEM WAS, if the senator said it was true, she had no reason to disbelieve him. In fact, the current revelation aside, Jessica admired Douglas Rothschild very much. A champion of the poor and the homeless, he had sponsored bills that would have provided shelter for the nation's poor, and when those had failed, had gone out to the private sector. And she knew she wasn't the only one impressed. It was those actions, the self-less, tireless generosity that Bennett focused on. Ambitious himself, but very much a liberal and a humanitarian, Bennett had worked side by side with the senator to see that the older man's goals were achieved. But his regard for the senator went much deeper than that. To Bennett, the senator was the father he had never had but had always wanted. The last Bennett had heard Suzette had admired him and looked up to him, too.

Which meant that all Jessica knew for sure was that Suzette had been afraid when she called Jessica for help, that the apartment had been ransacked, and that someone else had been there when she arrived. Clearly there was a cover-up going on, but instigated by whom? And why?

Gently the senator expressed his condolences once again. "I hate to leave, but I've got a roll call to get to."

"Of course," Bennett said solicitiously. "You take the limo. Jessica and I will grab a cab when we're ready to go."

"I'll see you at the funeral tomorrow," Senator Rothschild said at the door in a low concerned voice "Take care, both of you."

No sooner had he left than Bennett wrapped an arm around her shoulder in a chivalrous manner she suddenly found suffocating. "Jessica, listen to me—" he began "—you've been through a lot."

And there was still so much more to come.

Aggravated, she shrugged off his light, protective hold. "Stop treating this as if it's some calamity that will pass in a few hours or days if we just leave it alone. It won't! Suzette is dead. And I may have been the last person who talked to her! Dammit, don't you understand? I feel responsible." She *was* responsible. Helpless tears rolled down her face. If only they could turn back the clock and stop what had happened.

Bennett shook his head, disagreeing. "Suzette did this to herself," he pointed out calmly. "I know you don't want to believe it, but—all the facts point to it. Maybe whatever she was seeing Dr. Conti about was just too overwhelming for her to deal with. Maybe—maybe she just took those drugs because she wanted to escape for a little while. You know how reckless she was—"

That was true, but she had never messed with drugs. Not while Jessica had known her. Then she remembered the other shocking revelation. "I didn't even know she was seeing a psychiatrist." As close as they'd been, Jessica didn't understand why Suzette wouldn't have said something about that.

"Neither did I until the senator told me yesterday. He feels responsible, too, Jessica, for not seeing this coming, not noticing. He swears she wasn't distraught when she was at the office."

"But he—he believes it, doesn't he?"

"Like you, he doesn't really know what to think. No one wants to believe the worst, but on the other hand, sometimes people disappoint you."

Like Jessica's father, walking out on her when she was five. Like Bennett's, who hadn't even cared enough to marry his mother. No, life wasn't fair, and neither was this.

There was a possibility, however dim, that Jessica hadn't ever really known Suzette. "It hurts, me finding out about the psychiatrist this way. Why didn't she tell me? Why didn't she trust me if something was bothering her?"

"Maybe it wasn't something she could talk about. Maybe she didn't want to burden you."

"That's what friends are for," Jessica said fiercely, feeling tears sting her eyes.

"Then maybe she was embarrassed or saw it as a sign of weakness."

Angrily Jessica brushed away her tears. That she could believe. Suzette had always taken pride in her self-sufficiency.

"Look, you're welcome to stay with me at my efficiency here, if you don't want to be alone tonight. I'll sleep in a chair or something. Or if you want to be alone, I can get you a room at the Hilton. Whatever you want." Bennett was anxious to get out of the dead woman's apartment.

But not Jessica. Wiping away the frustrated tears with the back of her hand, she announced, "Thanks for the offer, but I think I'll stay here tonight."

"In Suzette's apartment?" He was aghast.

Jessica shrugged. "I'm the closest Suzette has to family. Someone's going to have to go through her things. The landlord is going to rent this apartment—" Her voice caught and she couldn't go on.

"Someone on the senator's staff can do that," he said gently.

"No. Suzette wouldn't want that." Jessica swallowed hard. "I'll do it." And maybe, just maybe in the process she would find some answers. Maybe she'd figure out where Suzette had put her manuscript and journal. Was it possible it was locked up in her suitcases? Suddenly Jessica realized that in the whole time they'd been searching Suzette's apartment, they hadn't come across any suitcases. And Jessica knew Suzette normally had two blue American Tourister pullmans stored in her bedroom closet. Where were they? Was it possible the manuscript and journal and notes were in those two pullmans? Since Suzette had been planning a trip to Ohio to finish the book, it made sense.

Aware that Bennett was watching her studiously, she tried hard to keep her demeanor casual. She knew he was concerned about her. But time was of the essence and she didn't want him getting in the way of her finding out what had really happened to her friend. She knew in her heart it wasn't a suicide, caused by a self-inflicted overdose, no matter what anyone else said!

"You want me to stay?"

"No. I'm exhausted, and I'm sure you are, too. But if you could pick me up in time for the funeral—"

"All right," he said finally with obvious reluctance. He clearly didn't agree with her choice, but knew she had every right to make it. "If you need me before then—" Hastily he scribbled his Washington address and phone number on the back of his business card. "You promise you'll call me?"

Jessica thought of the many years they had been friends back in Ohio, and of what Bennett had done for her when her own mother was dying. He might have unswerving professional and political ambitions of his own, but he was also kind and generous and loyal, sometimes to a fault. She knew that in the past four years he had begun to care about her, more than he should—or than she cared about him. She'd taken pains in the past not to lead him on, to make sure he knew that even though they were both grown up, it was still a friends-only type of thing with them. Apparently this incident had brought out the Sir Galahad in him along with his own possessive, protective feelings where she was concerned. She would have to take pains in the future not to let Bennett get any closer, or to give him hope where there was none. She valued his friendship; she didn't want him falling in love with her, because there was no way on earth she could return those feelings. There was something too ambitious, too mannered about him to suit her tastes. A relationship would prove disastrous, for both of them.

"I'll call you if I need you. But I think I'll just take a general inventory, decide if there's anything I want, and then start packing up the rest for charity." She had to find those two suitcases!

He gave her an odd look. "You're awfully calm now."

"I know. I was hysterical earlier. It's just... it's been a shock. I guess I'm overtired, that's all."

Wordlessly he touched her arm, his sympathy for all she was going through evident. "You're sure there's nothing I can do?"

Jessica shook her head slowly. *No.* There was nothing he could do. But she had plenty left for herself.

First and foremost was finding the copy of the block-buster manuscript. What had Suzette titled it? Jessica struggled to remember their conversations over the two-year period her friend had been working on and researching it. Suddenly the title sprang to mind: "Dreams of Glory." *Appropriate,* Jessica mused. The manuscript was supposed to make Suzette both famous and rich.

After letting Bennett out, Jessica searched relentlessly for the next three hours. The suitcases were not in the apartment. Neither were Suzette's purse, keys, or the ribbon from her portable typewriter. She also knew that Suzette kept a leather-bound personal journal secreted in a special place at the back of her bottom dresser drawer. It wasn't there, either. Frustrated and curious, she called the building superintendent, then the police. Neither had seen suitcases, the journal, or admitted to touching her friend's typewriter. The police did have Suzette's purse and keys, however—they had confiscated them at the scene and would keep them until the case was officially wrapped up. They estimated it would be another week before all the paperwork was finished. At that time they'd return the keys to Jessica, as Suzette had no other family.

For all Jessica could discover, the suitcases had disappeared into thin air—and Suzette's journal and unfinished manuscript right along with them.

The only positive find in an otherwise grim afternoon was an empty business envelope lying among a stack of bills on the desk. What it had contained was missing, perhaps tossed out as unimportant. Suzette no doubt had wanted to keep the envelope, because on it was the name of her agent: Tamara North, followed by a specific address in the heart of New York City.

Putting the envelope into her purse and snapping it shut, Jessica felt satisfied with her gleaning. She'd found some items gone that should have been in the apartment, but enough clues to work with. There was still the funeral to attend, then some tasks around town to take care of. But she consoled herself that afterward she could catch the shuttle to New York for a heart-to-heart chat with Tamara North.

Chapter Three

"You'd think they'd stop with the pictures. Enough already," Jessica murmured under her breath as the graveside service concluded. The camera crews from television networks and newspapers had been at the rural Virginia cemetery since the first limousine bearing Senator Rothschild and his family had arrived. They hadn't stopped filming since. And the incessant intrusion of the cameras and crews seemed ghoulish in the extreme to Jessica. Wasn't it enough that Suzette was dead? Did they have to turn even her burial into a media circus? she wondered on a new wave of grief.

"I know," Bennett consoled her, wrapping his arm securely around her waist and pulling her in to his side. He sighed heavily, then continued under his breath, "But what can you expect? She was on the senator's staff. A senator who may be the next president of the U.S. Her death was drug-related. It looks...very bad."

Jessica knew he was worried about the bad publicity, but then that was Bennett's job. He was responsible for seeing to the senator's continued good public relations—in his home state of Ohio, as well as occasionally in DC.

Jessica looked around. On the edge of the crowd of mourners, among the journalists, was one who really stood out. As far as she could tell, he was working alone. His Nikon pointed toward her, he snapped several pictures of Jessica and Bennett before moving on to photograph the senator's family. "Who is that?" Jessica whispered, inclining her head slightly in the photographer's direction. She didn't like the way he kept looking at her—in fact the way he studied everyone.

Bennett's mouth tightened unhappily. "That's Mark Gallagher. He works for *Personalities* magazine."

"You don't like him?"

"He can be trouble. From what I hear, though, he's mostly unreliable, always quitting his job to go off on a safari or mountain climbing in the Andes."

Jessica turned back surreptitiously. The man did have a certain rough-and-tumble quality to him. Though it was a funeral, he hadn't bothered to dress appropriately, but simply as if he was there to do a job unrelated in any way to the distress of the mourners present. In charcoal-gray slacks and multistriped blue, gray and white sweater under a leather bomber jacket, his appearance was both casual and somehow riveting. For a moment Jessica couldn't seem to stop staring or taking in the man who had made such a nuisance of himself during the somber proceedings. His dark blond hair was on the longish side, parted on the side and brushed away from his face to reveal a strong masculine forehead and straight dark blond brows. His face was ruggedly carved, the cheekbones high, the eyes arresting, the nose prominent and straight. The wide sensual mouth and stubborn chin only served to add more character.

Catching her glance, he held it momentarily. There was no kindness in his eyes. Only a kind of hardened curiosity that made her want to shiver.

She moved away, glad for once that Bennett had put an arm around her. "If he's so difficult, how is he able to work for a prestigious magazine like *Personalities*?" Trying to break into the upper echelons of the journalism world, it had been her experience that the elite jobs were very hard to get. And even harder to keep.

"Because the man's a sainted genius with a lens," Bennett muttered unhappily. "He makes even the least photogenic look good somehow." He sighed. "Remember that last layout on the senator and his family?"

"The one that hinted he might run for president next year?"

"Right. Well, Gallagher took the photos."

"They were good."

"Damn good," Bennett agreed, "though I wish to hell he weren't here today. This is the kind of national exposure the senator doesn't need."

And what about Suzette? Jessica wondered. What had she needed? Jessica couldn't stop the string of questions going through her mind. Why had Suzette been running back to Ohio? Of what and whom had she been afraid? And why hadn't she caught that plane . . . ?

"Jessica, hi." Craig Rothschild came up to say hello. Craig was the senator's only child and had dropped out of college after his freshman year. At the senator's request, he had begun working on his father's staff as a general aide. She had met him briefly during the last campaign, during the week or so when Craig had worked out of the Ohio headquarters. According to Suzette, the two Rothschilds had never gotten along. She, however, had liked Craig a lot, and feeling sorry for him, had tried in a roundabout way to take him under her wing. From Craig's swollen eyes and trembling hands Jessica could see that he was one of the few mourners there besides the senator and herself who were genuinely grief-stricken.

"Hi, Craig." She clasped his outstretched hands tightly, wishing there was something she could say that would make this easier for them all to bear. "How are you holding up?" she asked quietly, letting him know with a single compassionate look that she understood what he was going through and shared his deep grief.

"Okay." Craig swallowed hard. "It's been rough, though. Reporters everywhere, asking what we all knew about Suzette's state of mind. I keep trying to avoid them—my dad said he'd kill me if I talked to any of them, but—you know how it is. They're there, firing off questions, and before you can think, you—"

Bennett frowned, and taking Craig by the arm, hastily led him aside. "You didn't tell them anything, did you?" Bennett asked harshly.

Craig shook off Bennett's warning grip. "Like what?" he retorted fiercely, clearly disliking the public scolding. "That she got lonely sometimes, just like me?"

Jessica took a deep breath, about to intervene, when the senator and his wife walked up. "Craig, there you are. Your mother and I have been looking for you." The senator forced a travesty of a smile. "We're going to go back to the house now." The senator looked at Jessica. "We're having a wake—"

She nodded. "Bennett told me."

"You'll come, of course."

Jessica accepted, knowing she needed to be there.

"Maybe we can talk there." Craig whispered as soon as his father was out of earshot, giving Jessica a steady, meaningful glance. Jessica wondered suddenly what he knew. He seemed to be hinting at something, wanting to talk to her for a specific reason.

"Craig!" the senator commanded impatiently when he noticed his son had not followed them.

"Coming, Dad," Craig muttered irritably and with a final, almost pleading look at Jessica, raced off to join his parents.

Jessica stared after him, wondering what was going on between father and son. Was it possible Craig was somehow connected with her friend's death? Did he have an idea who might be?

She had no more chance to think about it, because Audrey Moore came up to her. The attractive thirty-five-year-old woman had been the senator's office manager for years. It was a well-known fact there had been no love lost between the ambitious twenty-six-year-old Suzette and Audrey.

"Ms. Lowell?" Audrey addressed Jessica formally, even though they had met previously during the senator's last campaign in Ohio. "My condolences. I understand you and Ms. Howar were very close."

"Yes, I loved her very much," Jessica said. *Maybe as much as you always seemed to hate her.* Suzette had said it was because Audrey had always been in love with the senator. Ignoring the fact the senator was married, Audrey had viewed the young, incredibly gorgeous Suzette as major competition for Senator Rothschild's attentions.

"Well, it's a tragedy," Audrey said finally, struggling for something honest to say.

"Yes, it is," Jessica snapped back harshly. She really wished people who did not grieve for Suzette hadn't come, never mind the appearances.

"Jessica?" Bennett interrupted her thoughts. "Our limo's waiting. We really should go."

Jessica saw Mark Gallagher watching her, though he wasn't photographing her this time. The man made her uneasy.

She turned to Bennett. "Yes. Let's go."

She wanted out of there. She wanted answers.

THE ROTHSCHILDS' HOUSE was filled to overflowing. Music played softly in the background, barely audible above the hum of voices and the clink of glassware and silver. While Bennett went off to speak to some reporters about Suzette, Jessica began looking for Craig. To her disappointment, she couldn't find him anywhere on the first floor.

She was about to head upstairs, when the handsome journalist Mark Gallagher appeared beside her. "Hi. I don't believe we've met." Camera bag over one shoulder, he extended his hand.

She took it reluctantly. "I'm Jessica Lowell."

"Suzette's friend. I know. I'm sorry. She spoke of you often."

Jessica paused, surprised at the casual affection in his voice. Although Suzette had known many people, she hadn't made that many genuine friends—mostly because her vast ambition and occasional abrasiveness put people off. Most people had never seen past that to the sweetness and caring Suzette was capable of, but apparently Mark had. "You knew Suzette?"

Mark nodded. "Not that well. We met at a party a couple months ago. I saw her a few times afterward." His eyes narrowed. "I know what they're saying about what happened to her, but she never struck me as the type who'd commit suicide—even accidentally." He took her hand, not giving her a chance to respond. "Let's go someplace where we can talk, alone."

Relieved finally to have someone agree with her, curious as to what he had to say to her, Jessica followed Mark up the stairs to the first empty bedroom, where coats were carefully stacked on the canopied double bed. The intimacy of the room, of being there with him, was overwhelming. Suddenly she wanted desperately to be in more neutral territory. Anywhere that didn't have a bed. Her mouth dry, she sputtered, "I don't—"

"Come on, it's the only place we'll have some privacy," he urged casually, as if it were the most natural thing in the world for them to be there alone together. Giving her no chance to refuse, he shut the door behind them with a soft thud.

What's done is done, Jessica thought.

Releasing his grip on her hand with the same studied casualness, he walked over to the window seat and gestured to the armchair beside it. "Want to sit down? You look a little tired, strung out."

She did indeed. All at once feeling immeasurably warmer under his compassionate, understanding gaze, she sat down. She felt in need of a strong shoulder to cry on, a man to lean on, if only for a moment. And for some reason Mark Gallagher seemed to fill that bill to perfection. But even as she thought it she pushed the idea away. She didn't need to get close to any magazine people...not when she felt as vulnerable as she did. She knew how they operated. *Anything for a story.* And the one time she'd looked directly into Mark's eyes at the cemetery, she'd seen only hardened curiosity, with no trace of the kindness and sensitivity he was exhibiting now.

"It was nice of the senator to pay for the funeral and host the gathering downstairs," Mark said quietly. He didn't seem to want anything from her at that moment but time out. Maybe a little intelligent conversation.

At his low-key attitude, Jessica again felt herself begin to relax. Whether that was a wise move or not, she didn't know. "Yes, it was," she agreed candidly. "Especially since Suzette didn't have any other family."

"Except you. And a few other people who cared about her."

"They just didn't know her, not like I did." *Yes.* Suzette had been flawed, but she'd also been very good. Very giving.

Mark was silent for a moment. When he spoke again his voice was low and gentle. "I understand you were the one who found her." Sympathy was in his voice and his eyes, but Jessica had been a reporter herself for long enough to know when she was being guided down the wrong path . . . subtly milked for a story.

She stood abruptly, her spine stiff. "I'm not going to be interviewed."

He stood too. "This isn't an interview." He caught her arm, his expression still gentlemanly, persuasive. "It's a friendly private conversation."

"Are you telling me your magazine wouldn't print a scoop if I gave you one?"

He was silent. "First of all I'm a photographer, not a writer. I just take the pictures."

Jessica uttered a short mocking laugh. "You're telling me you wouldn't share a scoop with a staff writer?" When he didn't deny it, she continued haughtily, "I didn't think you'd pass that up."

She turned away.

He caught her arm. "Look, I knew her," he said penitently, in a tone that had her turning around to face him, even though it went against her better judgment to look into those mesmerizingly candid eyes. "Not well, but I knew her," he admitted softly, honestly. "And something about this doesn't sit right with me. Okay? So yes, I wanted to talk to you."

Without warning, Jessica's legs felt as if they were made of putty. She sat down before she collapsed, staring at him all the while. *Funny.* He was the first person she'd met who seemed to share her gut-deep suspicion that some sort of cover-up was going on.

"You think something else was going on, too, don't you?" His look was hard, sharp.

"I'm not sure I should be talking to you." She resisted the urge to squirm.

He sat down again. "Somebody has to talk. Either that or her death goes on record permanently as a suicide." He leaned forward restlessly, his hands loosely clasped between his spread knees.

Jessica didn't want her friend's death considered a suicide. But she didn't know whether she could trust Mark or not, either. And that put a considerable damper on what she would or would not say.

"What did you see when you walked into that apartment?" He took charge of the conversation.

"I don't really remember."

His gaze was sharp, penetrating. "Was it ransacked?"

The hairs on the back of her neck stood up. She swallowed hard around the sudden uneasy lump in her throat. "What would make you think that?" Jessica asked nervously. Did he know about the sensational book Suzette had been secretly working on before her death?

"Nothing in particular," Mark answered casually, watching her carefully. "Except that apartments sometimes get ransacked when someone is murdered."

Jessica swallowed again, determined to give away nothing of what she knew, while at the same time learning from him everything he *did know—or suspect*. "Do you think—?"

"I don't know." He shrugged, his light green eyes never leaving her face. "That's why I'm asking you. From what I knew of her, Suzette Howar was not the type who kills herself. No, she struck me as someone who would fight to the death. And if that were the case—I mean, don't you think it's kind of strange you were assaulted, if nothing out of the ordinary had been going on there?"

The door opened without warning. Bennett walked in. "Jess, there you are! I've been looking everywhere for you." He acknowledged Mark coldly. "Gallagher, I would've thought you'd be downstairs helping yourself to the buffet. It is free, after all."

Mark grinned and got slowly to his feet. He met Bennett's searing glance with a cynical look that said he didn't care what Bennett or anyone else thought of him. "Maybe I will at that," he said laconically, rubbing at the back of his neck. He dropped his hand slowly and nodded at Jessica. "Nice talking to you."

"What did he want?" Bennett asked as soon as they were alone. Walking over to the door, he shut and locked it.

"Just information on Suzette's death." Suddenly Jessica was weak, unsteady. Her hands were shaking, her knees felt wobbly. She had a peculiarly light-headed sensation. She decided it must be a combination of hunger and fatigue. Either that or the mounting shock and horror of the last few days.

Was Suzette murdered?

It was a relief to Jessica to know someone else thought something evil was going on, yet it was frightening for her, too. Mark Gallagher wasn't a man she wanted to be in cahoots with. *Not now. Not ever.* There was simply too much going on behind those eyes of his.

"Look, don't talk to him again, okay?"

"Bennett—"

"The man's a vulture, Jessica. And you know how they are at *Personalities.* Anything to make a buck, they're just two steps above the tabloids, a halfway measure between sleazy details that sell and hard news."

"I know." Only about half of what that magazine printed was not libelous, Jessica knew. It was amazing they weren't sued more often.

"Look, I'm sorry if I snapped at you. I just...I don't want Suzette's memory or the senator hurt right now. So don't talk to Gallagher anymore, okay? You're in no shape to handle him right now."

He was right about that much, Jessica thought, taking the hand Bennett offered. She was in no shape to deal with Gallagher, not now, maybe not ever. He was just too wily. Too driven. And more trouble she didn't need.

"So what does this Jessica Lowell know?" Noah Chase asked hours later.

Mark stepped out of the shadows looming over the Potomac. "I don't know," he said roughly, infuriated that he hadn't gotten more out of her or been able to establish more than a very slight contact.

"Does she think her friend was murdered?"

Mark drank the last of his coffee. It was as cold and bitter as his mood. "She's not buying suicide, that's for sure."

"Anything else?"

What did he know about her? Mark wondered. That she had hair like soft spun gold? That she was tall and slim, with clear light blue eyes? That she'd seemed vulnerable to him, angry, suspicious and hurt—and on top of all that, wary as hell. "She doesn't trust anyone right now—" he said finally, deciding to leave it at that.

"Not even that small-town lawyer?" Noah pulled a small silver flask from his coat pocket. Unscrewing the lid, he took a small sip, then another.

"Bennett Agee? I don't know. He barely left her side. But she didn't seem to be confiding in him." Not as much as Agee would've liked, Mark thought. Because Agee had been first shocked and then jealous when he caught Mark alone with her in that upstairs bedroom.

"Did she confide in you?"

"No. Not much, anyway." Had he been given more time...a more suitable place...

"You'll have to change that," Noah counseled autocratically.

"Maybe easier said than done," Mark replied irritably.

Noah lifted an indifferent shoulder. "Would you prefer I assign someone else—?"

"No," Mark said swiftly before he could think. "I'll shadow her." This was his, *dammit*. He'd worked for years to get where he was, and no one—not even Noah—was going to deny him that now.

"You'll have to do more than that. You'll have to control her one hundred percent. Because none of this can get out, do you understand me? Because if it does, it could get very ugly."

Mark sighed. They both knew all the facts weren't in yet. And right now, *like it or not,* it looked as if Jessica Lowell was the key.

Noah calmed down enough to advise in the silky-soft voice Mark most detested, "Get close to her. Tell her anything you wish. Romance her. But get the job done."

Abruptly Mark crumpled the empty Styrofoam cup in his hand. Swearing at his boss, he said, "I get paid for my ability to infiltrate. Nothing else—"

Noah arched a dissenting brow, interrupting just as irascibly.

"Fine. See that you do just that." Slowly he replaced the flask in his inner coat pocket and met Mark's eyes. "There's no room for failure here, Mark."

Chapter Four

"Thank you for seeing me," Jessica said as she was ushered into Dr. Ethan Conti's private office.

"No problem." His expression sobered abruptly as he got up and pointed her to a chair that fronted his vast mahogany desk. As she settled in, he continued, "I'm sorry about your friend. I gather you and Suzette were close?"

"Best friends." Jessica was silent, for a moment just taking him in. The Washington psychiatrist wasn't at all what she'd expected. With gray hair at his temples, a lean aristocratic face and a tennis player's build, he had a friendly you-can-tell-me-anything air and a compassion for others that seemed to go soul deep. She guessed him to be in his mid- to late forties. He was dressed well in a suit and tie, but not ostentatiously so, considering that many of his patients were very wealthy—if she could judge by those she'd seen coming and going in the waiting room, anyway.

"Look, I know about patient-doctor confidences—" she began awkwardly. She didn't want to put him on the spot, yet there was much she had to know.

To her relief he understood. "In this case, because Suzette is dead," he said gently, "I'd like to do anything I can to set your mind at ease."

The depth of his compassion brought tears to her eyes. "They're saying it's suicide."

"I know." His mouth and eyes hardened stubbornly. "I don't believe that for a moment."

Her spirits soared. Here at last was hope. To have this evaluation from a professional person, the psychiatrist who'd been treating Suzette, meant Jessica wasn't alone in her indignation over the police verdict. "You don't?"

He shook his head defiantly. "Suzette was never in the least bit self-destructive. That was something I admired about her."

Jessica let out a slow breath and knotted her hands in her lap. "Then what do you think happened?"

"I'm not sure. Suzette started coming to see me about six months ago. She was under considerable stress—because of the book she was writing. You knew about that?" Jessica nodded and he continued. "Yes, she said you did. Admittedly, much of the stress was self-imposed, since she hadn't yet found a publisher for her work, but she was feeling the need to finish it, just the same."

"What advice did you give her?"

He gestured obliquely. "First of all, of course, to take it easy. To slow down."

"And did she?"

He bit his lower lip in apparent frustration. His eyes met hers directly. "You probably know as well as I what a dynamic woman Suzette was. No, she didn't slow down. She did ask me for a prescription for Valium." Again, Dr. Conti frowned. "I turned her down. I didn't think she needed tranquilizers half as much as she needed a friend to talk to."

Jessica felt a stab of guilt. She pushed it aside. "And you were that friend?"

"I was her doctor, but yes, I cared about her as a person, too. I care about all my patients."

Jessica could see that was true. "I still don't see how—" She paused and sighed at her vexation. Surely Suzette had possessed an extra copy of the manuscript. She'd probably put it somewhere for safekeeping—just on the outside chance of fire or theft. The question was where? Could it be in her safety deposit box? Or with her literary agent Tamara North in New York? "Did you ever see any part of the book she was working on?" Jessica asked impulsively.

Dr. Conti shook his head. "She never offered to let me read it. Do you have a copy of the book?" He leaned forward earnestly, his excitement apparent.

"No, I never read any pages, either."

"That's too bad." Dr. Conti frowned and sighed. "I was hoping maybe the manuscript would give us a clue as to what she was thinking before she died."

"It was apparently a self-administered combination of heroin and cocaine that killed her. I just can't believe she would willingly take those drugs, especially in combination. She knew how dangerous that was. And I can't accept the police theory that she committed suicide.... Suzette wouldn't handle problems that way."

Dr. Conti studied her silently, finally asking, "What else about this is upsetting you?"

It was reassuring to have someone understand her unwillingness to let this go without trying to figure out what really happened and why. Jessica turned to him, relieved to have someone to confide in. "Suzette called me the night she died. She was upset, but more out of fear than despair. She was going to catch a plane to Ohio and stay with me a few days. She even asked me to come to the airport and get her." Remembering the phone call, Jessica felt strung out and tense.

"But she never showed up."

Because she was already dead. "No, she didn't," Jessica said quietly, swallowing hard. Her feelings were in such turmoil. She was scared and sad and angry.

"And you feel guilty?"

"Yes. Very."

"Look, I know she was nervous about being found out about writing the book. She knew Senator Rothschild would be furious, if he ever learned of it. And there were others in his office that she felt resented her deeply in a professional sense."

"Are you intimating it was murder?" If so, he was concurring with suspicions Jessica had already had tenfold.

"I think the book—although I never read any of it—or maybe just the fact that she was writing one—could have threatened some people who had something to hide. Its existence would provide a motive for murder. On the other hand, Suzette was aware of this and she was also very good at keeping secrets. Except for you—as far as I know—no one else knew about the book."

"She talked to you about me?"

"Oh, yes. I know you roomed together in college. She talked quite a lot about you, as a matter of fact. She said something to the effect you were her best friend, that the two of you were like sisters."

"We were."

"I am sorry." His secretary buzzed him on the intercom and he glanced at his watch. She knew he had other patients to see, and that she had taken up more than enough of his time.

"Well, thank you. It's helped talking to you."

He spoke briefly to his secretary, reassuring her he hadn't forgotten about his next patient, then strode around his desk and unhurriedly showed her to the door. He paused abruptly. "Maybe I shouldn't ask, but...have you gone to the police with your suspicions?"

Jessica shook her head.

His glance narrowed. "Don't you think you should? I mean, if there's even a *possibility* of foul play here—?"

"That's just it. I don't have any proof." And until she found the manuscript, there wasn't much she could do. Until she could go forward with something concrete, she would just have to keep looking on her own. Jessica took a deep breath and met his gaze straightforwardly. "Thank you for talking to me, Dr. Conti. I really appreciate your candor."

At that his expression saddened. "Let me know if there's anything more I can do." As he finished, his eyes were kind. "I'd be glad to help in any way I can. If you discover proof there was foul play," he said, his conviction on this evidently as strong as hers, "I want to see something done about it, every bit as much as you."

No SOONER had Jessica returned to Suzette's apartment than the doorbell rang. Looking through the viewer, Jessica saw Mark Gallagher, camera bag slung over one shoulder and a serious-looking young woman beside him. She was wearing a press badge on the lapel of her blazer that read *Personalities*.

Before Jessica could decide what to do, the bell rang again. With a reluctant sigh, she unlocked the door and swung it open.

Mark wasted no time on amenities. "Can we talk?"

"I don't—"

"Please," the young woman with frizzy red hair and big horn-rimmed glasses intervened. "Mark says you're one of the few people who genuinely seemed to like the deceased. We really need a few positive comments from you to balance the article we have to publish."

Under those circumstances, Jessica didn't see how she could refuse. "All right. But I don't want to talk long."

"You won't have to," the young woman promised. "By the way, I'm Natalie Jackson. And I guess you've already met Mark."

"Yes, we've met," Jessica said through stiff lips. She wouldn't soon forget how he'd maneuvered her into an upstairs bedroom, all for the purpose of seeing if there were any skeletons in Suzette's closet. She was sure of that now.

They all took a seat, Mark and Natalie on the white and mauve floral sofa, Jessica on an overstuffed mauve armchair adjacent to them. "Are you saying Suzette committed suicide?" Jessica asked. She wanted to know right off what they planned to print in their article.

Natalie and Mark traded telling glances before Natalie answered warily, "That is the official cause of death."

"She didn't commit suicide," Jessica muttered, as much to herself as anyone else.

Natalie raised her brows as she turned on her recorder. "What did you say?"

Jessica was silent, deciding after the fact that she'd already said more than enough. She also knew her slip was more Freudian than not—her subconscious knew it wouldn't hurt to have more sleuths on the murderer's trail. Maybe between the three of them, even if they were working separately, they could dig up something the police had overlooked.

"Maybe we should start with how they knew each other," Mark broke in gently, getting out his camera.

Relieved to have something easier to discuss, Jessica said, "We were roommates in college. Both of us were journalism majors and interested in becoming writers, so although we were quite different in personality, we had a lot in common and got along very well."

"You were roommates all four years?" Natalie asked.

"Yes. And we continued to be friends, after she'd moved to DC to work on the senator's staff."

"She was a research assistant there—?"

"Yes. And she also helped research and write some of his speeches. Suzette had a flair for the dramatic. The senator loved and appreciated it."

"Was that all he loved about her?" Mark asked, putting together his camera.

Natalie poked him in the side. "Hey, I'm supposed to be asking the questions." She turned back to Jessica. "Was that all he loved about her?"

In other circumstances, their Laurel and Hardy routine would have been funny. Now Jessica only found it annoying. "I don't know what you mean," she answered stiffly. "I think you'd have to ask the senator."

Turning on the camera's flash, he moved away from the sofa and got down on one knee. Mark shot one photo after another of Jessica, moving and shifting until he had photographed her from all angles. Jessica sat still, trying very hard to ignore him, but it wasn't easy when he made her move and pose so the sunlight was sifting through her hair "just so."

"We have already asked the senator," Mark continued eventually. He stopped messing with his camera long enough to look at Jessica. "He didn't have much to say except the usual stuff about Suzette being a valued employee." Mark was clearly not impressed by the politician's diplomacy.

Jessica thought about the personal interest Senator Rothschild took in all his employees, and realized he was only protecting Suzette's memory by being effusive but vague.

"Is there anything you can tell us that will shed light on what happened?" Natalie asked, breaking into Jessica's thoughts once more.

Jessica shook her head, deciding she wouldn't tell them about Suzette's phone call or her plans to flee Washington and seek haven secretly in Jessica's home while she finished her book. "No. I just know she was mostly a lighthearted, if ambitious, personality."

"Are you implying it might have been murder?" Natalie asked, her curiosity now rampant.

Jessica shrugged and looked the nosy reporter in the eye. Maybe some good would come of this yet. "You tell me."

ONCE SHE'D PIQUED their interest, Jessica couldn't get rid of the *Personalities* people quickly enough. No sooner had they reluctantly left her than she started out on her next errand.

Fortunately, Gloria Rothschild was home when Jessica arrived at the senator's residence, and the senator's wife agreed to see her.

Jessica was ushered into the den by a uniformed maid.

"Darling, come in," Gloria greeted her with unusual hospitality. She stood, smoothing her loose-knit sweater over her slim hips, unconsciously showing off a trim figure that was honed to a perfection only immense sums of money could sustain. "You poor, poor dear," she continued expansively, waving her martini glass in the air. "You've been through such an ordeal."

"Yes. Hasn't she though?" another woman said.

Gloria waved a manicured hand toward her friend, sitting unobserved in a corner wing-backed chair near a fireplace. "You know Pamela, don't you, dear?"

There wasn't an American alive who hadn't seen Pamela Fieldler on the evening news, espousing one cause or another, Jessica thought. She'd given speeches against apartheid, acted as a spokeswoman for environmental causes, and worked to provide privately funded shelter for the homeless. "Senator Fieldler's wife. Of course. I'm glad to meet you," Jessica said, extending her hand and crossing over to her.

The slight woman with the bobbed dark hair and cornflower-blue eyes took it and smiled at Jessica. Barely noon, both women were sloshed to the gills. If Jessica had to hazard a guess, Gloria's dark brown eyes could hardly focus.

"Won't you join us in a drink?" Gloria gestured to the pitcher of martinis. Swaying slightly, she made her way to the bar and rather sloppily poured herself yet another drink.

"Um—I can't," Jessica temporized. She followed that with a smile. "I'm taking antihistamine for an allergy, and I can't mix the two."

"Oh, of course." Gloria said. Padding back to the couch, she stretched out on the red leather and took another lengthy sip of her martini. "Well, have a seat anyway, dear, and tell me what's on your mind."

I want to know what you know or suspect about Suzette's death, Jessica thought, knowing that of course she couldn't say that. So she contented herself with thanking Gloria—quite sincerely—for the wake she'd held in Suzette's honor.

"Oh, darling, think nothing of it. I was happy to do whatever I could under the circumstances."

"Unfortunately there are a lot of ugly rumors going around—" Jessica began.

"Don't I know it," Gloria said darkly, looking fixedly at the olive in her glass. "Douglas is very upset. For anyone to think that someone on his staff—Suzette especially—would ever use drugs—" She shuddered, unable to face the implications, political or otherwise.

"Oh, fudge to the rumors," Pamela said drunkenly, downing her own martini at breakneck rate. "And for that matter to all husbands, too."

Gloria, the more sober of the two, sat up abruptly and leveled a censuring glance at her friend.

Remembering abruptly that Jessica was in the room with them, Pamela sobered slightly. Hiccuping, she pressed quieting fingers against her lips. "Sorry." She looked at Gloria, then at Jessica "You'll have to forgive me. I'm down on the world today, men in general, husbands in particular."

Gloria nodded. Apparently deciding some explanation was in order for Jessica to even begin to understand what was going on and maybe even sympathize with them, said, "Pam gave another interview. Her husband Russ is furious, naturally—again. I suppose you saw it—*Nightly Interviews*. Three days ago—"

Now that Gloria mentioned it, Jessica had seen it. And she'd been impressed. "Yes. You came out very strongly for more government-sponsored social programs. Considering the current political climate, and the fact your husband is a staunch Republican, that was a very courageous stand for you to take."

"Not as far as he's concerned. Russ thinks I've ruined him."

Gloria sighed. "You know the rules, Pam. Seen and not heard. Good political wives smile and shake hands and never, never express a political opinion or idea of their own. It doesn't sit well with voters."

"Keeping mum doesn't sit well with me."

Pamela Fieldler was one of the most outspoken wives on Capitol Hill, Jessica knew.

"Mrs. Rothschild?" the maid interrupted them. "A Mr. Mark Gallagher and Ms. Natalie Jackson from *Personalities* magazine are here to see you."

Suddenly both women became alert, aware of their condition. Whatever the lapse in judgment they'd allowed themselves, it faded, and faded fast. "I can't see them," Gloria replied. "Not now. Not anytime soon. Have them—have them call my social secretary in a few weeks."

Or as soon as the brouhaha about Suzette has died down, Jessica thought.

"And Jessica, you'll have to excuse us, too," Gloria said in a tactful but firm voice. With her fingertips she pushed at the tousled mass of her curly, frosted hairdo. "I'm afraid you've caught Pamela and me—" she looked protectively at her friend "—at a very bad time."

A very vulnerable time, you mean, Jessica mused, disappointed. But no sooner had her spirits fallen, than she forced herself to gather her courage to go on. One way or another, she would get to the bottom of this yet.

Chapter Five

"Did someone pay you to follow me, or are you just doing it on your own?" Jessica asked, more than a little perturbed by Mark Gallagher's presence.

Mark grinned as he fell into step beside her. "A little of both." He'd followed her cab from the Rothschild residence to Capitol Hill.

"Where's Natalie?"

"She went back to the office to begin transcribing her notes on the Suzette Howar story. We go to press in another two days, so there isn't much time for her to pull things together."

Nor did *she* have much time to discover the whole truth, Jessica thought to herself, depressed. With an effort, she kept her demeanor unreadable. Simultaneously, she tried not to notice how enticingly windblown Mark looked, his dark blond hair all mussed and begging to be combed back into place, his cheeks ruddy from the cold. She shook off the unwanted romanticism and fixed steady blue eyes on his face. "And where are you headed?" she asked briskly. Hopefully in a different direction.

With a telling look that said he'd accurately read her thoughts, and in turn was amused by them, Mark answered in a casual tone that mocked hers to a tee, "I'm on my way to get a few photos of Senator Rothschild, maybe of some of the people in his office." He watched her speculatively, continuing dryly, "Where are you off to?"

As if he didn't know. "The same place," she said coldly. She wasn't sure what it was about him, whether it was the charming voice that could come and go as swiftly as the wind or the unfathomable light green eyes, but she didn't trust him. Didn't trust him at all.

"Why haven't you gone back to your job in Ohio?" He seemed to think that since the funeral was over, it was the natural thing for her to do. And it would've been, had Suzette's death been above suspicion.

"Someone has to stay and take care of Suzette's things." She was irritated to find that on this point anyway, his thinking was clearly aligned with Bennett's. He'd also urged her to get out of town. Instead, Jessica had taken herself to the nearest department store, bought several new sets of clothing as well as the necessary toiletries and a suitcase, and settled in for a brief, if—she hoped—extremely productive stay at the Harrington, an older moderately priced hotel within walking distance of the mall and a short cab ride from Suzette's apartment on Connecticut.

"You could hire someone to do that for you," he pointed out neutrally. They moved into the Capitol building, toward the side that housed the senators' offices.

She was helpless to prevent her chin from tilting stubbornly. "I know I could, but I'm not."

Without warning, he took her arm and as effortlessly and gracefully as if they were dance partners on a stage, backed her up against the closest wall. His eyes were now a deep, shimmering green. Suddenly she had a feeling he saw and knew too much. "What is it you don't like about me?" he asked gently, his soft voice acting like sandpaper on her already ravaged nerves.

She swallowed hard around the tightness in her throat and ignored the unsettled feeling in her middle. "How about everything?" Ignoring the pounding of her heart, she pushed him deliberately aside.

To her surprise he didn't try to detain her again but merely followed her lead, keeping pace beside her as easily as if they'd been walking and working together for years. Shoving both hands into the pockets of his khaki pants, he said, "So. What did you learn from Gloria Rothschild?"

Jessica kept her eyes straight ahead. She refused to acknowledge the physical attraction that she felt between them. Reacting with a haughtiness that belied the faint flush coloring her cheeks, she replied, "That, my dear colleague, is none of your business."

"Okay then." The smile in his voice matched the genial one on his face. "*Why* did you go to see her?"

She stopped abruptly and swung around to face him. "Look, do us both a favor and try and get this through your thick head, Mr. Gallagher. What I am doing and why is none of your business. Nor will it ever be."

His grin broadened. *Want to bet?* it seemed to ask.

She wasn't quite sure why he was following her so eagerly. It suddenly seemed more than just for his magazine story. But she wouldn't let herself pursue it. Turning on her heel, she wheeled away from him and went on.

Jessica was still blushing when she reached the senator's door. Fortunately neither Bennett nor the senator was in at that moment. Audrey Moore was.

Impatiently she listened to Jessica's censored account of her meeting with Dr. Conti. "Look, it doesn't matter how or why Suzette got those drugs. The fact of the matter is, she's dead. I think you ought to let this go." Irritated, she tugged at her sweater, pulling it down over her plump midriff.

"I can't. Don't you understand? If she was murdered—"

"Look, I didn't like her," the homely office manager admitted. "And I'm not going to start pretending at this point that I did. She was an ambitious back-stabber who used everyone in her path. She also liked to party. So maybe she used drugs, too."

"You don't believe that," Jessica disagreed heatedly, not caring for the moment who might come in. She pointed an accusing finger at Audrey. "You would have known if she was on drugs. Everyone here would have. It's not that hard to tell when someone's using!"

Audrey turned a little pale at that and didn't dissent.

Seeing she was getting somewhere, Jessica lowered her voice and continued compellingly, "Please understand, I'm not trying to cause trouble for the senator. But for my own peace of mind, I do have to get to the bottom of this. Now, do you know of any enemies she might have had?"

"No."

"The day she died. Did she come in to work that day?"

"No, she never showed up. Never called, either." Audrey had apparently found that unconscionable.

"Was that usual?" Jessica pressed.

Audrey hesitated, for the first time looking scared. "No."

"Do you have any idea what was going on with her?"

"No, and no one else did, either. She buttered up the senator all the time, but as for the rest of us—Bennett, me, everyone else on the staff—it was as if we didn't exist. Oh, sometimes she'd get real nosy, and ask us all sorts of personal questions, but other than that—"

She'd been surreptitiously interviewing them for her book! No wonder they'd all resented her. They'd sensed she was using them, and in a way she had been, all for her own gain.

Jessica could see Audrey's patience was at an end. "One more thing. Did Suzette ask for time off recently? Did she tell you she was planning to take a vacation?" Had anyone known she was planning to fly to Ohio to hide out?

"Of course not," Audrey said, aggravated again. "Suzette knew the senator is very busy this time of year. There was no way, no way she could ever have gotten vacation time now. None of us could."

But Suzette had been willing to take off anyway, Jessica thought. She'd been scared for her life—not depressed and intent on taking it. Jessica wasn't any closer to the truth.

"I THINK YOU SHOULD go back to Ohio, and the sooner the better," Bennett said several hours later in her hotel room. He'd come to see if he could take her to dinner. "This refusal of yours to accept reality isn't healthy. In fact, it's downright self-destructive."

"Thank you very much."

"Jessica—" Now he was contrite.

"Dammit, Bennett, she was my friend."

She exhaled slowly, willing herself to relax. More than anything, she wanted Bennett to understand. "I can't just leave her death this way. If it had been your friend

who died, if it had been the senator, would you be able
to just let it go?''

''There's no comparison between the senator and
Suzette,'' he said coldly.

But there was, Jessica thought. Maybe more than he
knew. Both had lusted after fame and power and for-
tune. Both had loved being in the limelight and
constantly wanted more. Yet they'd wanted to do more,
too. They'd wanted to make a difference, the senator
through his social programs, Suzette through the statement made by her book.

''Jessica, you've got to stop this and go home—''

''And if I don't?''

''I won't have you harming the senator.'' His words
sounded suspiciously like a threat, and a chill went down
her spine.

''You really mean that, don't you? Your first alle-
giance is to him.'' She was hurt now, and disillusioned.
She hadn't expected him to abandon her.

''Jessica, don't force me to choose—''

''I'm not going back, Bennett, not until I've satisfied
myself about what happened to Suzette.''

Clearly curious and thwarted, he stared at her. And
then she knew that their friendship had come to an end.
It didn't matter how long they'd known each other; the
simple fact of the matter was that they had changed,
drifted apart. *Yes.* She had needed him and needed him
badly when her mother was dying. He'd been a compa-
triot in the small town, but now they were just strangers
with completely different goals.

''Jessica—''

Before she could stop herself, she found herself saying, ''I want you out of here—now.''

She could see that he knew when a decision was irrevocable. "Don't do anything you'll regret," he warned severely, then let himself out.

JESSICA KNEW the only thing she would regret would be letting Suzette's death go as it was. *No.* She had to know the truth. She didn't care what it cost her in terms of time or emotional energy. What was important was clearing Suzette's name.

And the first way to do that was to gather evidence, establish a motive—prove to the police that someone had a motive for wanting Suzette dead—a motive that was tied to the book she'd been writing.

She booked a flight to New York for the morning. But first she called Tamara North's office in New York. A secretary intercepted the call, claiming Mrs. North wasn't in after 4:30 p.m. But when Jessica stated her business, there was a pause. "Wait a minute," the young woman said. Several minutes later she returned. "Is eleven o'clock tomorrow morning okay?"

Jessica jumped at the opportunity. "Of course. That'll be fine."

"YOU HEARD about her death?" Jessica asked, as soon as she'd been shown into the agent's plush New York office. The cool efficient secretary had ushered her in, then returned to her typing in the front office.

Tamara North smoothed the chunky gold jewelry around her neck. A chicly dressed woman in her late thirties, Tamara had jet-black hair and olive skin. Her eyes were dark—almost black—and evasive. "Yes. Of course. It was on the network news." If the agent felt any emotion, she wasn't showing it.

"I know you were representing her and that she was writing a blockbuster novel about the Washington scene, an insider's view of the Capitol," Jessica continued.

"It wasn't a novel," the other woman answered briskly. "It was a biography of Senator Rothschild, in anticipation of his upcoming presidential bid."

Jessica was stunned. "Suzette never said anything about a biography," she observed, regaining her voice. Fiction had always been her first love. "Can I see the manuscript?"

"No. That would violate client confidentiality."

Frustrated by Tamara's lack of cooperation, Jessica protested, "Suzette's dead—"

"All the more reason to let the project end here and now," Tamara said firmly.

Jessica studied her curiously, wondering why Tamara was lying to her and why she looked so frightened. "You don't want to capitalize on the sensationalism surrounding Suzette's death? Surely anything she wrote would sell, no matter what shape it's in. The public is very interested in everything about Suzette's life-style, reporters are coming out of the walls to get details of her life—any details. I know her book wasn't finished yet, but you could sell excerpts or have the ending ghostwritten."

Tamara grew even paler. "All I have now is a proposal in a very rough stage."

"You never read any pages?"

"No."

"Not even a rough draft?"

"No!"

She was lying again! Why, Jessica didn't know. "Suzette told me her agent had read the first three hundred pages, that you were very excited about the work and were pushing her to finish."

"Then she was misleading you both about that and about writing a novel," Tamara said flatly, her black brows rising in visible aggravation. "Because I never had anything to do with a blockbuster novel she may or may not have been penning. Now if you'll excuse me, I have to get back to work." Looking pale and strained, she led the way to the door.

Fast—and a flop, Jessica told herself as she walked along the streets of Manhattan minutes later. She would've thought the trip not worth her while, except that she was sure Tamara would have refused to talk on the phone. At least Jessica had learned one thing. Tamara North was lying. And she was frightened. *But why?* Had someone threatened her, too? The way they'd threatened Suzette? Did she suspect Suzette was murdered for what she was doing? Or was Tamara somehow involved in the killing?

JESSICA WAS still puzzling over Tamara North's obvious duplicity when she arrived at the airline counter to check in. "What do you mean, I'm not booked on the return flight to DC? Of course I am!" She'd picked up and paid for her ticket that morning.

The ticket agent looked at her as if she'd lost her mind. "You *were* on it, but then you canceled."

"No, I didn't."

"Well, someone did. We've already credited your Master Card with a refund."

She stared at him in mortification.

Without warning, her name was called over the public address system. "Jessica Lowell, report to the information counter. Jessica Lowell, please report to the information counter."

The ticket agent shrugged. "Maybe there's your explanation."

"I hope so," Jessica snapped. If not, there was going to be trouble, the likes of which he'd never imagined.

Pivoting sharply on her heel, she walked briskly to the information desk. "Oh yes, Ms. Lowell, we have a package for you." The clerk retrieved an eight- by eleven-inch manila envelope and handed it to Jessica. "There you go."

"Who brought this?" The envelope was light.

"I don't know. To tell you the truth, I didn't see. We were very busy this morning. When I looked up, the package was here, with a typed note pinned to it telling me what flight you were on, with what airline. I started paging you about forty-five minutes ago."

Sighing with frustration, Jessica walked over to the nearest chair and sat down. Impatiently she tore open the envelope. Inside was a one-way ticket back to Ohio for that very day with another airline. And along with that, a small sample-sized white plastic vial of Estée Lauder's Swiss Performing Extract, the facial moisturizer she used. Jessica wondered what was going on. Was this Bennett's idea of a going-home present, or a convenient effort to get her out of the way, and hence out of the senator's hair?

Curious, and a little angry, Jessica looked around her. If Bennett was at the airport, he was nowhere in sight. Frowning, she opened the vial, and tipping it over quickly, she tapped a little of the liquid onto her hand.

To her dismay, it wasn't the fragrant moisturizer she'd expected, but bright red and thick. It was blood, and she'd just poured it all over her hand.

With a startled gasp she let it go. The container bounced as it hit the floor, splattering more blood across the linoleum. Beside her a woman screamed.

Suddenly it was more than Jessica could take. She felt herself pitching forward, as the roaring in her ears increased, then everything went black and she slid into a dead faint.

THE FIRST THING Jessica saw when she opened her eyes was Mark Gallagher's face. Then she noticed she was in a strange room, the sounds of the airport in the background. "Thank God," he said with what she could only hope was genuine relief.

"I told you it was just a faint," the woman in white said imperiously. She withdrew the ammonia capsule from under Jessica's nose. "She'll be all right in a moment."

"Where am I?" Coughing and choking on the noxious ammonia fumes, Jessica tried to sit up and was promptly pushed back down.

"The first aid station at the airport," Mark answered softly.

She stared at him. Although he'd taken his hands away as soon as she acquiesced to his demand to rest, she could still feel his warm, gentle touch on her shoulders. "What are you doing here?" Her throat was unaccountably scratchy and impossibly dry, lending a husky quality to her voice.

Mark's light green eyes grew as caressing as his voice. "I work in New York, remember? At *Personalities* magazine."

She quelled her reaction to his nearness. "Right," she replied tartly. "And you just happened to be in the airport the exact moment I fainted."

"Okay, so I followed you." He grinned unrepentantly at his confession of nosiness, then all the amusement faded from his eyes. "Good thing, huh?" he commented.

Jessica wasn't sure. At that moment, she didn't know whom she could trust. "If this is your idea of a joke, Gallagher—" She struggled to sit up again, and this time he let her.

"It isn't a joke," he hit back. "And you can relax, at least for the moment, because I didn't have anything to do with it."

She stared at him warily, biting her lip. "How do I know that?" How did she know anything?

He kept his gaze level with hers. "I guess you'll have to take my word for it." His tone was brusque and slightly angry.

Jessica sighed and ran a hand through her hair. If he wasn't innocent, he was putting on a damn good show. She sighed again. Should she ask him for answers? Since he'd been there, he might know something. "Who did this to me?"

Mark's powerful shoulders rose and fell. "I don't know," he said, apparently honestly, his hypnotic eyes on hers. "I wish I did, though. It'd make a hell of a story." Again he gave her that roguish grin.

Her stomach churned, and churned again. Pulse racing, Jessica stared at him uneasily.

"Look. You want to file a police report?" Mark Gallagher asked, suddenly serious again and doing his best to be helpful.

She nodded slowly. If someone was out to scare her, she wanted it all on record.

The policeman wasn't happy that Jessica had no idea who had done this to her. Nonetheless, he took the small bottle and bagged it as evidence. "Ten to one there won't be any fingerprints on it, but we can test and type the little bit of blood left in the bottle."

"You'll let me know the results?" Jessica asked.

"Yeah. It'll take a couple of days though. In the meantime, I suggest you be careful. This could all be a nasty trick, just meant to scare you. But it could also be more...much more...,"

Evidence of a psychotic mind, Jessica thought, shivering again.

The cop's eyes narrowed as he focused on her unease, and sensing all that she was withholding, he pressed her again. "You sure you don't know who did this to you? You can take your educated guess, you know. Youse don't have to have any proof."

"No, I don't know," Jessica said. Unless it was the same person who'd murdered Suzette.

The cop frowned. "You doing anything to make enemies?"

"I think the question is, what hasn't she done?" Mark injected dryly.

The cop and Mark exchanged looks, as if both were vowing to do everything in their power to protect Jessica and simultaneously discover what she was up to. "Anything else youse wanna tell me about?" the cop asked kindly.

"No, I'm fine." Jessica said. She just wanted to go back to Washington, DC. Now, more than ever, she was sure she was onto something.

The nurse insisted that Jessica drink a glass of orange juice before she left. Mark stayed, walking with her out of the lounge and back toward the ticket counter. "You've been very good, Mr. Gallagher, but I don't need a bodyguard."

"Call me Mark. And I saw how much you don't need a bodyguard." he muttered.

She turned to him accusingly. "For all I know, you could have been the one who engineered all this, just to get me to rely on you."

"You're right. It could've been me, but it wasn't. It's not my style."

She could believe that. If he were after a woman, he'd want to take her head-on, in a full frontal assault. He'd probably want her to know it was him, too, rather than maintain anonymity.

She rubbed her temples. None of this made sense.

"Still feeling bad?"

"Lousy."

"Anything I can do?"

"Yeah, stop following me."

To that he made no response, neither denying nor granting her request.

"This was a warning, you know," he said finally, sounding more like Bennett than she wanted to admit. "Maybe you should heed it, and use the ticket back to Ohio."

The only problem was, Jessica couldn't do that. "No," she said firmly. She knew she had to discover the truth. She owed it to Suzette and she owed it to herself. Only when she knew who was behind her friend's death and saw them put away behind bars would she feel safe again. The incident in New York had proved that.

Bloody warning or no, she was going to continue until she had every answer she needed.

To Jessica's dismay, Mark Gallagher lined up behind her at the ticket counter. "I've told you all I'm going to."

"Maybe," he said affably, pulling his wallet out of his hip pocket. "But in any case, you're not the only reason I'm going back to DC."

"No?" She looked at him, her disbelief evident.

He gave her a lopsided smile not mirrored by his eyes. "I've been assigned to photograph Craig Rothschild."

"In conjunction with the senator?"

"In a roundabout way." He studied her briefly, looking mysterious. "You haven't heard, have you?"

She stared at him, sensing very bad news. "Heard what?" she asked unable to hide the dread in her voice.

"Craig Rothschild's been arrested. Happened early this morning. It's already been on every network news program—but I guess you haven't been near a television set."

"Arrested? Craig?" The sensitive nineteen-year-old who looked incapable of harming a fly? "Why?"

Mark compressed his mouth grimly. "He was caught trying to buy heroin and cocaine from an undercover cop."

Chapter Six

"So how is Craig?" Jessica asked Bennett the moment he let her into the efficiency apartment he kept for his stays in DC.

"How'd you hear about it?" Bennett asked, looking glad to see her despite the unpleasant events of the day.

"I ran into Mark Gallagher." She deliberately didn't say where or when. "He told me about it."

Bennett yanked off his tie with a vicious motion. "Damn leech. He was at the jail this evening, you know, snapping photos as Craig was released."

"I'm sorry."

"Yeah, well so am I. Craig has no right to be putting his father through this right now. He knows the senator may run for president next year. And now . . . criminy, none of this is looking good."

"Bennett?" She took a deep breath. "Do you think there's a connection between what happened to Suzette and what happened to Craig last night?"

"What kind of connection?" He looked at her with easy affection, reminding her of how long they'd been friends. He wasn't perfect, neither was she, but they had always been there for one another in the past. Part of her didn't want the easy accessibility to stop. Another part of her was wary of his new priorities and ambitions—goals that were every bit as strong as the powerful, influential man he worked for. Behind him, the microwave buzzer sounded. Bennett walked over and pulled out a steaming entrée.

Jessica watched as Bennett tore off the plastic cover. "Is it possible they were on drugs—both of them?" She didn't want to even consider that possibility, but she knew she had to look at this from every angle if she expected to figure anything out.

He shook his head. "Craig said he was just trying to figure out why she'd overdosed. He went there looking for answers, and now *he's* on the hot seat. The damn fool kid. Do you want some of my dinner? It's just a frozen entrée—stuffed peppers and Spanish rice, but I've got others in the freezer."

"No thanks."

"Some juice then?"

"Sure." Bennett walked over to the refrigerator and pulled out a jug of orange juice as she settled down at the kitchen table.

"What are you going to do?" She watched as he poured her a drink, then fixed himself some ice water and gulped down half of it in one swallow.

"It's already been done." He wiped his mouth with the back of his hand. "The senator is pulling a few strings. They're going to make a deal—he'll plead guilty and get a community service rap instead of jail, along with voluntary counseling. The conviction won't look good on his record, especially added to the fact he's already dropped out of school, but there's not much more the senator can do—particularly since the wire services were so quick to pick up the story. The case against him is ironclad." He sighed. "At any rate, he'll be out of sight for the next few days. The senator's having him taken into seclusion. Even I don't know where he'll be. So that should keep the reporters from finding him.''

"I'm sorry. How's Gloria taking it?''

"The usual.'' Bennett sat down at the table and dug into his dinner as if he hadn't eaten for days. "She's drowning her sorrows in a bottle of vodka.''

Not a very good example to set for her son, Jessica thought. Especially when he'd just been picked up for possession of controlled substances.

Seeming to guess at the turn of her thoughts, Bennett gave her a sharp look. "About what happened the other day.'' He put down his fork. "I want you to forget what you saw at the Rothschilds' house. Gloria and Pamela both were not at their best.''

In other words, the fact they were drunk was not to be aired. His assumption she'd divulge that to anyone stung her. "I don't want to hurt anyone, you know that,'' she countered self-righteously.

"But you are, just by refusing to drop this investigation of yours.'' He frowned again, then spoke to her as one friend to another. "I've said it before. I'll say it again. I think you ought to go back to Ohio, Jessica. The sooner the better.''

She took a deep, shaky breath and gathered her courage. "Is that why you sent me that package?'' Jessica asked.

Bennett looked genuinely confused. "What package?''

They'd known one another too long to lie to each other. She could swear he was telling the truth. But if it hadn't been him, who had it been? Suzette's murderer? Was it possible the murderer was now after her, too?

"Nothing—" She stood up. The fewer people who knew she'd been to New York to see Tamara North, the better.

"Jess—"

"I've got to go."

He walked her to the door. "You're not leaving town?" He was disappointed.

"No, not yet." She still had far too much to do. And seeing Craig Rothschild—when he came out of seclusion—was only one item on her list.

"LOOK, MS. LOWELL, we understand you're upset about your friend's death—" Sergeant Kendall began the following morning. "But you won't help me," Jessica said aggravatedly, anticipating what he was about to say.

"What do you expect me to do? I mean what proof do you have? There are no papers, no notes, no half-finished tell-all book to back up your claim."

"And the police department doesn't have them."

"Like I told you, when we got there, except for your friend being dead—by the way she was in her bed, not on the living-room floor, as you remember—nothing else in the apartment was amiss. You were hysterical.... You don't remember any of this?"

Jessica shook her head, feeling confused once again. It was all such a blur, as if it had happened to another person in another lifetime. Very vaguely she could remember bits and pieces; being attacked when she walked into the apartment, then nothing until later, when she was being helped into an ambulance; the staring faces of neighbors and passersby, but that was all. She had no other memories until she awakened in Potomac General. Even with the time that had passed, with her diligent efforts to try and remember, nothing concrete came to her mind. She supposed her amnesia supported Bennett and the senator's claim that she had suffered an emotional collapse after discovering Suzette's body. Maybe Jessica had been drugged, maybe she hadn't. But there was no way for her to prove that now. Her unsubstantiated claims only made her seem all the more hysterical and irrational.

"We don't have any papers, nor did we see anything resembling a book or notes for one." The police officer paused, unable to hide his skepticism. "You're sure your friend wasn't making all this up to impress you?"

"No. I never saw them, but she told me about them. She said she had reams of notes. But I'm also sure—" because of the nature of what she'd been working on "—she kept them locked up or hidden. Never out in plain view. Her address book and her journal are also gone."

"We never saw those, either."

"You're sure? Isn't a missing address book suspicious to you?"

"Ms. Lowell, an address book can be lost or misplaced as easily as any personal item. Besides, I was there the whole time the investigation was conducted. I'm telling you, it looked like an open-and-shut case to me. Your friend committed suicide, whether it was accidental or not. It's happening with increasing frequency all over the country, when done by mistake."

"How can you be so sure it was accidental? Were there other needle marks on her arm? Was there damage to the inside of her nose? No, of course not."

He clamped his lips together until they were white. "I didn't want to get into this, but you leave me no choice. The reason we're so sure is because we have photographs of your friend in clandestine meetings with a Washington pusher, Vinnie Forsythe. He's a known supplier for a lot of the users from the upper classes."

For a moment Jessica was so stunned that she couldn't speak. No wonder the police hadn't tried very hard to investigate! They thought they knew all the answers, when in reality they knew as little as she did. *No.* Only Suzette had known what she was up to, and why. "Where can I meet this Vinnie Forsythe?" Jessica snapped, her patience at an end.

"You can't," the sergeant said grimly. "He's gone underground."

"So what's next?" Mark Gallagher asked several hours later, as he watched the uniformed workers carry the furniture out of Suzette's apartment.

Jessica turned to face him. She'd been wondering when he would turn up again. "They're taking Suzette's furniture back to the rental company."

"She didn't own it?"

"No."

"What about the rest of her personal belongings?"

"I've packed them up." Jessica suppressed the grief welling up inside her. There'd be a time for mourning later, but not now. "Aside from her clothes, which I'm donating to charity, she didn't have much. She liked to travel light."

Mark studied her, seeing beyond the surface composure. She ignored the compassion in his eyes.

"Does this mean you're going home?" he asked, keeping his tone carefully casual.

Jessica nodded. Although she'd spent the last twenty-four hours calling every Forsythe in the book, she hadn't found a single lead to point her to Vinnie. "I don't want to, but I have to admit there's not much more I can do here. I've talked to everyone who'll talk to me, including the police." She was also hoping there'd be something for her in Ohio—a letter from Suzette, some message from beyond the grave. The journal, something. If not, she'd already devised the next course of action. She'd comb her memory, question people who'd known them both, visit old haunting grounds, dig for any small clue that would point to where Suzette had hidden her personal papers, papers that would reveal why she had died. And Jessica was more and more certain that Suzette had hidden them. Why else would the papers evaporate into thin air? Even if the originals had been stolen, copies had to exist somewhere. Jessica knew her friend too well to believe otherwise.

"And?" Mark had to prompt, reminding her he was still there.

"And nothing. They think it's an open-and-shut case."

"And you don't."

"Right now it doesn't matter what I think." Determined not to let him know she still had hopes that some answers lay in Ohio, Jessica watched as they carried the last end table and the bed frame down the hall. She paused to sign a form saying the movers had been there, and accepted a pink receipt.

Mark waited until the movers had gone before he inquired, "So when are you leaving?"

"Tomorrow. I've got a flight out in the morning."

"Want to have dinner with me tonight?"

Jessica stared at him irascibly, trying to figure out what he was getting out of this. "Why? Planning to get me drunk and see what you can worm out of me for the magazine?"

Her sarcasm made him angry. "I don't work like that," he snapped back gruffly. "Though if I did—" without warning his voice lowered to a mesmerizing drawl "—you'd be the first person on my list to debauch." He gave her a smile that had her tingling all the way to her toes before he sobered again. "Seriously, I just want to talk."

"About Suzette?"

"Too much of what happened to her just doesn't add up. I need to talk to someone. I thought you might, too."

Jessica was silent. She needed an ally. She was also aware he might have uncovered something in his snooping that she didn't already know. "All right," she said finally. At this point she had very little to lose. And maybe everything to gain. With his *Personalities* connections, he had the entrée to the innermost corridors.

Besides, he'd said he was Suzette's friend. Maybe it was time she put that claim to the test.

"So how well did you know her?" Jessica asked, as soon as they'd settled into the family-style Italian restaurant down the street.

"Well enough to know that she liked hard rock and white wine. That she almost never wore pants if she could help it. She said her legs had gained her entrée to more places than she could count, and she doubled that when she wore spike heels."

Jessica caught her breath. He had summed up Suzette very accurately. But then, he and that writer had been doing a profile on her for *Personalities*. "Who was her favorite author?"

"She never could decide between Jackie Collins and Mark Twain."

Right again. "Did you ever date her?" The question slipped out before Jessica could censor herself.

Mark fixed his eyes on Jessica as he answered quietly but candidly. "Her tastes ran strictly to the rich and powerful. She also wasn't my type."

Jessica was silent. Suddenly she was too tired for words, emotionally exhausted by the events of the last four or five days. "Is what you just said going to be in the magazine, too?" Would Suzette be portrayed as some man-eating social climber-adventuress?

He shook his head. "No. The editors have decided to really play up the drug angle—the fact that cocaine and heroin are everywhere nowadays."

"You sound like you disapprove." That pleased her.

He shrugged. "I think the writer is way off track, but hey, what do I know? I'm only a photojournalist, hired to record the people around her on film."

Jessica understood the limitations he felt. She felt limited too in what she could do, and that gave them a powerful—if temporary—bond. She forced her mind back to Suzette and the mystery surrounding her death. This was her chance. "And what have you found out in doing that?" she asked casually. "Anything I should or would want to know?"

Mark shrugged, his eyes holding hers intently. "Your friend Bennett doesn't hold her in very high esteem."

He seemed to be accusing Bennett of something. Jessica felt herself becoming as prickly as a cactus again. "Bennett was with me that night," she snapped. So Mark could stop short of whatever he was forming in his mind.

Mark's brows rose in interest. "The two of you are involved?"

He cares who I'm seeing. "No. We're just friends."

"I see."

Did he? She wondered. And she wondered why she cared so much what he thought of her, when she didn't even know him.

Getting back on track, Mark continued. "I also think Audrey is a very possessive woman."

That was true, too. Jessica took another sip of her wine. "I know what you mean. Audrey never really has tried to hide her jealousy of Suzette's talent and beauty." She was also very protective of the senator. If she'd discovered anything about the book...

"People have been known to kill for less."

It was a chilling thought. Jessica put down her fork. "Wouldn't someone know something or suspect Audrey if that was the case?"

"Not necessarily."

"There must be other suspects."

"Like who? As far as I can discern, Suzette wasn't really close to anyone in DC except the people in the office and the senator's family. And they all have alibis— every single one of them. For instance, Senator and Mrs. Rothschild were at a state dinner at the time of her death. I know because I was working there that night, shooting a layout for the magazine. Craig Rothschild, whose recent drug arrest gives me cause to wonder, was at a Young Republicans' meeting across town. The rest of the senator's staff was at a birthday party for one of the secretaries. Audrey's the only one who doesn't appear to have an alibi, although she says she felt ill and went home alone to rest."

"As much as I want to find someone to hang this on, I still don't believe Audrey could've managed to forcibly administer a speedball. Suzette was too smart to be talked into something that risky."

"Yeah, well, something happened to her—something you claim was totally out of character, and I for one would like to know why."

So would I, Jessica thought. Feeling a rush of grief and frustration, tears blurred her eyes. Determinedly she blinked them back. She hadn't broken down yet, not even at the funeral, and she wouldn't do so now.

"I'm sorry. I didn't mean to upset you." He reached across the table and covered her hand with his.

"It's all right." His touch was reassuring in ways she didn't want. Feeling the need to be alone, to remain apart, Jessica withdrew her hand.

The waiter returned with their dinner. The rest of the meal passed swiftly. In an effort to suppress her emotions—she knew she was on the verge of a crying jag—she drank more wine than she was accustomed to. But she didn't realize just how tipsy she was until they were getting ready to leave.

She swayed slightly on her feet. Mark looked at her. "Thought so," he said under his breath, slipping a hand beneath one elbow to steady her.

"Then why didn't you stop me?" Jessica asked, feeling unnecessarily irritable again.

"Because you looked like you needed the respite," he added gently. "Even a temporary alcohol-induced one."

He was right about that, too.

The cold night air hit her with bracing intensity. As they walked toward the Harrington Hotel, where Jessica was staying, her head began to clear. She felt more depressed than ever.

Noticing, Mark said, "Maybe you'll feel better when you go back home."

"I'll feel better when I find out what happened to her," Jessica muttered beneath her breath. Then to her horror, as the irreversible fact of her friend's death hit her, the tears she'd been suppressing for days began to fall. She wiped them away with the back of her hand. To no avail. They kept falling. Mark was silent beside her, his arm tucked securely under hers. But when they reached the building and she was still crying, he turned her to him without a word, then in the shadows held her against him until the worst of the storm had passed.

When she finally wiped her face, Jessica was extremely embarrassed. "I'm sorry."

"Don't be. She was your friend. You cared about her. There's nothing to apologize for."

Nodding, Jessica moved away. With a sodden wad of Kleenex in one hand, she fumbled in her bag for the key with the other.

"There's something else I didn't tell you," Mark said. "Something you should know." His tone was deadly and quiet.

Alarm swept through her in numbing waves.

"That pusher who sold Suzette the drugs, Vinnie Forsythe. I talked to him earlier this afternoon. He's not the most reliable source. He's been in and out of psychiatric hospitals since he was a teenager, but he confirmed to me the fact that Suzette had been a regular customer of his for the last month. But she wasn't buying cocaine or heroin. Just lots of street Valium."

"Did Vinnie Forsythe say anything else?" Jessica asked tensely.

"Only that she had a lot of questions for him every time they met, about how much money he made pushing, things like that."

Jessica was silent. Maybe Suzette had been taking Valium as a way to calm down, to anesthetize herself from whatever was frightening her. But she hadn't needed to go to the street to get a prescription tranquilizer. She could have gone to any number of doctors in town and gotten that legally. So there had to be a reason she'd gone to Vinnie, a reason she'd been asking all those questions. Maybe it was a way of getting research for her book. She'd always been fascinated by all facets of life in the fast lane. Maybe there's been a pusher character in her book, and she'd been looking to try and give him "life."

Jessica looked at Mark's grim countenance. "You think it's possible Suzette did inject herself, don't you?"

He shrugged, obviously as confused and disturbed as she felt. "Suzette cornered me at a party a few months ago and told me that she had been hearing from other staffers on the Hill how to mix drugs. She wanted to know as much as possible about all of them. She also wanted to know my opinion, if I'd ever experimented myself or knew of anyone who had—"

"Have you?"

"No," Mark said roughly, plainly aggravated she'd even ask. "To both questions."

"Which leaves us where?" Jessica asked, even more depressed. How she wished she had Suzette's journal!

"I don't know." Mark was quiet for a minute, too. "Part of me rejects the theory of suicide, because a survivor like Suzette would never do anything that stupid. Everyone knows that speedballs kill. But I also know how much she wanted to live in the fast lane. Whatever, why ever," he finished savagely, "it was a stupid, senseless way for her to die."

Chapter Seven

Jessica thought about what Mark had had to say on the flight home. It was still on her mind when she went to her neighbor's to pick up the mail and the paper. If only Suzette had given her some pages of the manuscript, some proof she had been working on a tell-all book. Something that would establish motive and give the police something to go on, she thought, opening her front door. But she hadn't, partly because she'd been shy about anyone reading what she was working on, and partly because she hadn't wanted Jessica to read it until it was polished and perfect.

To Jessica's satisfaction, her house in Spring Valley was much the same as it had been when she left it. A two-story frame building half a century old, the house had first belonged to her grandparents, then her mother, and now Jessica. Modestly furnished, the white house with the pine-green shutters was clean and spacious. Area rugs decorated the polished wooden floors. The dark blue and wine-red furniture was overstuffed and comfortable, the calico priscilla curtains were made of a coordinating print.

Jessica watered her houseplants and sank onto the sofa to read her mail. *Bills, bills, and more bills.* She'd been hoping there'd be a letter from Suzette for her. To no avail. In fact, the only thing of interest was a letter from the Publishers' Clearing House. Jessica smiled, remembering how Suzette used to tease her about every sweepstake offer that arrived in her mail. To her ex-roommate's amusement, Jessica had entered the Publishers' Clearing House contest every year since she was old enough to fill out the form. *Including this year.* Jessica frowned, remembering she had already been solicited by them a month ago and had sent in her entry along with a subscription for *Redbook*. She'd never known them to send her a duplicate entry form before.

As she started to tear open the envelope, Jessica's glance fell on the Scotch tape on the back over the original seal, and what looked like a doctored address on the front. Eagerly she finished opening the envelope and examined the contents. Inside were the usual stickers and contest rules, along with a small handwritten note from Suzette. "I should have known you wouldn't leave a cold trail," Jessica murmured, recalling her friend's able mind. Excited, Jessica read her friend's last message to her.

Dear Jessica,
I'm really scared. You know how much I wanted to hit the jackpot? Well, I've stumbled onto something more horrifying and un-American than I ever thought possible. And the conspiracy seems to reach several levels.

Remember the good old days when we were roommates at Miami and talked every day? Ever wish we could go back or that things were as simple as they were that one resort summer?

"I'm relying on you to draw your own astute conclusions. Before all else, go to the post office, find out if you have any registered mail...."

Jessica's hands were shaking as she finished reading the letter. Suzette had to have been very scared, even paranoid, to have sent her a letter in a doctored piece of junk mail. She also clearly felt she was "on to something" and wanted Jessica to know the truth, too—if only by following the trail of clues Suzette had obviously set up in the letter. A trail only Jessica, with her intimate knowledge of their past, could decipher.

Jessica sighed, remembering how Suzette had always been the first to organize a scavenger hunt, the first to come up with the answer in even the toughest game of charades. Would Jessica be able to solve the riddle her friend had left for her as a way of speaking to her from beyond the grave? Would anyone else?

One thing was certain. Suzette had been right to sense her life was in danger. Now Jessica had to believe her death had been no accident.

But what had Suzette stumbled onto? What was Jessica expected to discover?

"WELL, HELLO, Jessica, what great timing you've got!" Melissa Crider said from the other side of the Spring Valley post office window.

"I take it there's a package for me?"

"Registered, too. From Washington, DC. You'll have to sign for it."

Standing on tiptoe, the postmistress retrieved the package from a shelf behind her and slid it across to Jessica. "When was it mailed?" Jessica asked calmly, catching the return address of S. Howar on the mailing receipt.

"Um, let's see. About ten days ago. Came while you were out of town. Couldn't deliver it of course, 'cause this was something you had to sign for personally, it being registered and all."

"Thank you for being so conscientious." Jessica smiled, the package already in hand. She cradled the brown-wrapped package to her chest, then opened it. Inside were about one hundred pages of a typewritten manuscript.

"Oh, you're welcome."

Jessica dashed out to the car, the manuscript in her tote. Wanting to read it right away, she headed for home, then changed her mind and decided she'd be better off reading the pages in a safe place. Somewhere quiet. She headed for the library in nearby Xenia, and taking the package with her, went to the reading room upstairs. It was nearly deserted as she settled down at a corner of the table.

Soon she was totally engrossed in what she was reading. It was the first third of "Dreams of Glory."

Suzette had indeed been writing a novel. As a writer herself, Jessica could see certain things that needed fixing—there wasn't enough detail or physical description, for instance, but she could also see the enormous potential the manuscript had, right down to the nitty-gritty detail of what it was like to work as a research assistant for an influential senator with presidential ambitions. The main character was named Daisy, a leggy, vivacious blonde, clearly modeled after Suzette herself.

Daisy was impressed by the devotion of the staff to the senator, and his to them, but she also found an excessive amount of bickering and back-stabbing among the staffers, and thought the cutthroat atmosphere disturbing and counterproductive.

Daisy, like Suzette, was fascinated by the Washington cocktail scene. She spent as much time with reporters and lawyers and influential lobbyists as she did with politicians, later chronicling everything she'd learned for the senator in informally written reports or by talking to him privately. The senator, pleased with her ambition and inventiveness, rewarded Daisy with better assignments—which also often earned her the jealousy of other staffers.

Daisy was also captivated by the mixture of drive, power and compassion that characterized almost all the senators she met—and equally disturbed by the life-style of some of their wives. They either had obvious problems with chemical dependency, were obsessed with their weight and looks to the exclusion of all else, or behaved almost like Jekyll and Hyde. One minute they were the perfect political wives, the next running off without a word—only to return later as if nothing had happened, as if they hadn't caused a stir by taking off on a whim, leaving their husbands in the lurch.

The first section of the manuscript ended with Daisy determined to have a closer look at some of the marriages, to find out what this Jekyll and Hyde behavior meant.

Finished, Jessica put the typed pages aside. Was this why Suzette had been killed, because she'd been about to try and publish a roman à clef of the political world? Because she'd dared to talk about ambitious staffers or peculiar behavior among some political wives? About how she'd sleuthed for the senator at cocktail parties and social events? Or was it something darker yet, something to be revealed in the next section of the book? Jessica knew only that she had to find those pages.

"I THOUGHT I told you to keep your girlfriend in line," Senator Rothschild growled.

Bennett swallowed nervously. He knew what a pain Jessica had been, but the two of them went back a long way, longer than he'd served the senator. Automatically he leaped to her defense. "First, she's not my girl-friend. We're just—buddies."

The senator's eyes softened. "I thought she depended on you."

"She did." At least when her mother had been sick. Then they'd been closer than he'd ever dreamed possible. But after Jessica had gotten over her grief, she'd begun to withdraw from him and the confines of their relationship. Bennett had tried to give her room, tried to let things ride. But for the first time in his life he'd been made aware that there was a possibility he might lose her. And he didn't know what he'd do without her.

"You know, this whole mess would be a hell of a lot easier to handle now if she were your wife," the senator mused pragmatically, sighing. "Then at least you'd have some say-so in what she did or didn't do."

Bennett was silent. He knew, privately anyway, that the senator felt it was the man's job to assume the position of head of the family. He also knew Jessica would never be less than any man's equal partner, and that might present a problem for him if he and Jessica were ever to get together. Because unless Bennett ultimately had the final say-so and called all the shots, then the senator and some of his other influential friends would privately consider Bennett to be "henpecked"—a fate worse than death for any politician or aide, especially these days when "overly influential" wives were being criticized for "helping" their husbands make policy decisions. "I'll keep her out of your way," Bennett promised.

"Make sure you do." The senator paused. He looked at Bennett thoughtfully, a troubled expression on his face. "What does she think happened to Suzette, anyway? I'm not sure I buy the suicide theory, either, but as for what else it could be...what does Jessica think? Has she confided in you?"

"She hasn't said anything concrete," he admitted, embarrassed. Restless, he headed for the bar and poured himself a stiff drink.

The senator watched him down the brandy. "But she's still digging around?" he asked unhappily, wishing, as did Bennett, that Jessica would just leave it alone and let them all get on with their lives.

"Yes, although as far as I know she hasn't managed to piece together anything yet that makes sense." Bennett took another long swallow of brandy. "Once the shock of Suzette's death passes, I think she'll calm down. After all, she's already gone back to Ohio."

The senator puffed on his pipe. He looked at Bennett, the strain of the last few days showing on his face. "Thank God for that." Silence. "You've got to keep her in line, Bennett. Because if, even inadvertently, she creates any more of a scandal for me, she'll pay the price, too. You understand what I'm saying?"

Slowly Bennett nodded, wishing fervently the nightmare would show signs of ending. First Suzette dead of an overdose, then Craig arrested for buying drugs. Gloria drinking. It was a public relations nightmare. He tipped his glass up and drained it. "She won't betray you," he promised.

The senator drew his brows together warningly, reminding Bennett he hadn't gotten where he was by being weak-kneed. "She'd better not," he growled. "Because if she does, I'm warning you, there will be a price to be paid."

VINNIE FORSYTHE was one of the first people to see *Personalities* as it came off the Washington newsstand. He was both disappointed and relieved his name wasn't mentioned in the article on Suzette Howar. He wanted to be famous, but he didn't want to be prosecuted for having sold her the heroin and the cocaine.

No. Jail was not for him.

He'd been there once, and barely gotten out alive. If he had to go in again... He shuddered, repressing the thought.

Turning up the collar on his coat, he headed back to the walk-up where he was currently hiding out. Not nearly as luxurious as his usual digs, it had heat and a roof over it. As well as an army of roaches and several large-sized rats.

Vinnie sighed. Because the cops were looking for him—they wanted to take him in for questioning about Suzette Howar's untimely demise—he couldn't go out and make the usual sales. Moreover, his supplier had refused to give him more stock.

Except for that Gallagher fella, whom he'd only talked to because they had several criminal friends in common, he hadn't seen anyone in three days—not since he'd been advised, by someone close to Craig Rothschild, that it might be politic of him to go into hiding.

The walls were getting to him, closing in.

If only he could get to one of his many bank accounts throughout the city. If only he had more cash. He could go someplace warm, someplace exotic. Somewhere nice and rich to wait it out, instead of being cooped up in this hellhole called low-income housing—which, by the way, he was currently renting illegally at twice the usual price. Feeling frustrated and restless, Vinnie stood, stretching his long legs, then smiled as an idea slowly formed in his mind.

Maybe there was a way out of this situation, after all. This was a scandal, right? A big enough one to possibly send him to jail. Thus far, only *Personalities* magazine had benefited. But now...now that was about to change.

Because he knew a lot.

And he just bet that knowledge was worth money to someone. Buckets of it. After all, Washington was full of prominent people who were wealthy as sin—public figures, who would have much to lose if the truth came out.

The question was, *how to get to them?* The usual route... well, that just wouldn't do. He would have to find another source, a roundabout way to tell his targets exactly what was on his mind. And genius that he was, Vinnie knew just where to start....

WHEN JESSICA FINISHED at the library, she headed for the nearest copying service. In a matter of minutes, she copied the first hundred pages of Suzette's manuscript. That done, she took one copy to her safety deposit box at the bank, the other to the carryall she had with her. From there she headed straight for Miami University, the place where she and Suzette had met and spent most of their "good old days" together. Logically Jessica decided that had to be where Suzette had hidden the journal and remaining manuscript pages mentioned in the cryptic letter, one of the few places specifically named.

The drive took forty-five minutes. Jessica arrived just as the students were heading to their four o'clock classes.

After parking in the visitor area, she headed for the freshman quad. She'd only graduated four years ago but she felt as if she'd been out of school for an eternity. She passed the casually dressed preppies and moved easily on cement walkways between the ivy-covered red brick buildings of Georgian design.

Passing the freshmen's residence halls she came to a gnarled tree, where Suzette had once suggested they leave notes for each other. A glance into the hole showed it to be covered with leaves. No notes, no letters, no journals. Jessica looked around with a sigh.

Maybe the answer was in their old dorm. She walked swiftly to the three-story red brick building and ducked inside. Finally locating a resident assistant, she explained she was looking for a package that might have arrived, either for or from Suzette.

The woman looked at Jessica, assessing her. "And you say she's not a student here?"

"Not anymore."

"Then why would a package be sent here for her?"

Because she needed a safe place for her journal, Jessica thought. Sending it to the school would get it out of sight for awhile and buy time until it was returned to the addressee. "It's kind of a scavenger hunt. A—a puzzle between some alumni. I don't expect you to understand—"

"That's good, 'cause I don't," the R.A. said with a smile, "but hang on. I'll have a look around." She came back minutes later. "I'm sorry. I can't find anything. I've asked everyone who might know. Nothing fitting that description, or even anything remotely mysterious has come in either this semester or last."

"Thanks anyway—"

"You might check the campus mail room."

Jessica grinned. Now there was an idea. "Thanks, I will."

Unfortunately, Jessica's search there proved equally fruitless. Determined to find the journal, she went on to the other three dorms across campus where she and Suzette had lived. Nothing there. Nor was there a safety deposit box listed in either Suzette's or Jessica's name at their old bank in town. Feeling very depressed and discouraged, Jessica turned and started back to her car. And it was then, when she was walking down East High Street, that she thought she saw Mark Gallagher standing in front of the Miami Co-op Bookstore. She blinked and looked again.

To her frustration, a surge of people had come out of the store. By the time she could see again, Mark—or the man who had looked like him—was nowhere in sight.

Feeling a shudder of apprehension slide down her spine, Jessica moved slowly toward her car.

Mark wasn't here in Ohio. She knew for a fact no one had followed her to Miami, because the roads between Oxford and Spring Valley were two-lane country highways, cutting across acres of farmland and empty fields and running through small towns with only one main street. *No.* If someone had followed her to Oxford from Spring Valley, she would have noticed. And no one had.

Therefore, this had to be her imagination, Jessica chided herself sternly as she got back into her car. She was just getting paranoid. She had to get a grip on herself. She couldn't afford to let herself panic. Not when it was so important that she keep all her wits about her.

"So where did she go?" Noah asked several hours later over the phone.

Mark took a deep breath and exhaled slowly. "To the university where she and Suzette went to school."

"Figure out why?"

"No, although if I had to guess, I'd say she was searching for something."

Noah paused. "You've got her covered?" he snapped.

"There's a tracking device on her car," Mark confirmed grimly.

"So wherever she goeth—" Noah chortled, clearly delighted.

"We'll know."

"Good." Noah paused. "You won't let her get away with anything, will you? You know how important it is that we keep this quiet."

"There's no chance of anything getting out. Believe me," Mark reassured the other man bluntly, "she's just not that clever." *Or a good liar, either.* Whenever she fabricated, he saw it immediately in her eyes—the way they darkened, or in the way she averted her gaze and took shallow breaths. *No.* With her racing pulse and her quicksilver emotions, she was an easy mark, he thought with a fixed smile.

She wasn't easy to understand. But he promised himself that before this crisis was over, he'd do his best. There wouldn't be a thing he didn't know about Jessica Lowell. Not a thing.

Chapter Eight

"Have dinner with me tonight," Bennett began later the next afternoon when he stopped by the *Spring Valley Sentinel* to see her. He had returned to coordinate a newsletter drive on the senator's behalf. He'd stay a week or until it was finished, then return to the senator's office in Washington. Two weeks here, two weeks there; his scheduled never varied.

Jessica looked up from her typewriter. Four-thirty; the small office had emptied fifteen minutes earlier. "I can't. I've got to stay late and finish up several articles I started before I left town."

Bennett pulled up a chair across from her. "You're still angry with me, aren't you? For not being more supportive of you back in Washington."

Seeing he wasn't going to go away, she stopped typing. Putting her hands on either side of her machine, she said wearily, "Look, I really don't want to talk about it."

"I think we need to. Jessica, I know Suzette's death was hard on you. And I'm sorry you're hurting."

She believed he didn't want her to hurt. "But you're not sorry Suzette's gone, are you, Bennett?" she asked quietly.

Bennett stared at her for a long moment. Finally he shrugged. "You want the truth? In retrospect I think she was a very selfish, single-minded woman who only had her own best interest at heart. I also think—and believe me I know this sounds hard-hearted—that the senator's better off without her. And you, too, though I doubt you'll see it that way."

He was right. It did sound cruel, impossibly so. "That's correct. I don't see it that way, Bennett." Furious he didn't share her grief, Jessica pushed her chair back from the desk.

Bennett sighed. "Now you're mad at me."

"What did you expect?" she snapped back.

His face clouded; clearly he was hurt. "Wait a minute, Jessica. You asked me what I felt. You're the one who pushed the issue." That was true; she knew he respected her too much to lie to her; that wasn't the way their friendship worked.

"I know." She ran a weary hand through her hair. "I'm sorry I snapped at you, too." It wasn't even Bennett she was angry with, it was herself. She was furious that she couldn't figure out where Suzette had placed her journal or the remaining portion of the manuscript, and though she'd been up half the night mulling over possibilities and replaying Suzette's message to her, nothing had come to mind. Nothing she hadn't already checked out at the university the day before.

"Jessica?"

"Maybe we should just agree to disagree on this."

"Okay." Briefly he looked hurt that she couldn't be more understanding of his point of view, but apparently he was prepared to push that aside. "About dinner—"

"I can't, Bennett. I'm sorry. I've just—I've got too much work to do. I'll probably be here for several more hours."

"I understand. I've got catching up to do here, too." He paused in the doorway, the look on his face reminding her of all they had been to one another. "You'll call me if you need anything?" he asked softly.

She nodded. "I promise." But she also knew there was very little he or anyone else could do. The puzzle had been left to her. She had to solve it. She had to find the rest of the manuscript and the journal to be able to figure out what Suzette had been on to that had gotten her killed. No one else could do that.

Jessica worked for another two hours, forcing herself to write up the usual mundane news: weddings and funerals, the community calendar, the results of the elections for the local 4-H club, the latest farm report. She stopped at the gas station and the grocery on the way home, so it was nearly seven-thirty by the time she pulled into her driveway.

Gathering a bag of groceries into each arm, she started up the walk. Juggling her purchases, she managed to open the door.

She moved inside easily, unmindful of the darkness, until the toe of her shoe hit a solid object in what should have been a clear path to the kitchen.

She paused, swallowing hard. Her heart pounding, she put the bags down where she stood and backed up until she reached the lamp closest to the door. Reaching over, she turned on the light.

She gasped as she surveyed the damage. Sofa cushions had been ripped open, the furniture upended. Drawers were open, the contents of her bookcases scattered across the floor. Thank God, she'd kept the extra copy of the manuscript with her all day, stuffed in the bottom of the oversized tote bag she routinely carried instead of a purse.

What if the burglar was still here?

Panic gripped her, a roaring in her ears, she whirled toward the door, intending to run. And it was then she saw him, his tall silhouette framed in the open doorway, blocking her exit.

Jessica opened her mouth to scream.

Mark Gallagher cursed and covered the distance between them in two short strides, the storm door banging shut behind him. His hand came up to cup her mouth and stifle the hysterical sounds. "Stop it! Screaming won't help. I just arrived myself. Why don't we just call the police?"

Slowly he let her go.

Jessica watched him warily, her heart pounding. Her mouth was dry, cottony.

"Where is it?" He glanced around him impatiently.

"Where's what?" She felt a little faint. And she still didn't trust him.

"The phone."

She pointed obediently. "It's over there, by the fireplace."

No sooner had he turned away than she started to edge toward the door. But Mark saw her and swiftly caught her wrist. Before she could open her mouth again, he put the phone into her hand and dialed 911.

Immediately someone came on the line. The dispatcher took the necessary details and told Jessica a police car would be over immediately.

Slowly she replaced the phone. Since he had helped her call the police, it was unlikely he meant her any harm. She began to relax. "You want to sit down?" he asked, surveying her emotionlessly. "You look like you could use a drink. Better not touch anything though, if you can help it. They'll probably want to dust for prints."

Jessica sat on the sofa, but only because her legs suddenly felt as if they wouldn't support her even one second longer. "Are you okay?" He bent closer, looking into her face, and she could have sworn that in that second his eyes were very kind.

Kindness would be her undoing, she couldn't afford to cry. Numbly she nodded. Looking away from him, she finally managed to croak, "I'm just shaken up." This was too much like the scene at Suzette's apartment.

Tense moments passed. As Jessica's mind began to clear, she wondered at the coincidence. Mark Gallagher didn't belong in Ohio, never mind at her house at precisely the moment she discovered there'd been a break-in. She looked up at Mark sharply, wanting answers. "What are you doing here?" she snapped. "And why have you been following me?"

He straightened casually. Watching the color fade anew from her cheeks, he gave her a twisted smile of ridicule. "I haven't been following you."

Now that was a lie! "I would have sworn I saw you at Miami University yesterday, in downtown Oxford!"

He nailed her with a judgmental stare. "I don't know what you're talking about."

Oh, yes. He did. And she wasn't going to leave him alone until he told her the truth. She balled her hands into fists and jumped to her feet, demanding again, "The truth, Gallagher. *What* are you doing here?"

Although she approached him menacingly, he didn't move away from her but rather stood his ground with his hands shoved into his pockets. Suddenly they were very close, close enough for her to inhale the spicy fragrance of his after-shave. "I just got into town this afternoon. I was assigned to take some new photos of the Rothschilds in their home here. The story, remember? I wondered how you were doing. As long as I was in town, I decided to try and see you. I tried to call you from the airport, but there was no answer."

"But you stopped by anyway—"

"Because I had something to tell you. The New York police have been trying to get in touch with you. Apparently you forgot to give them your Ohio address and number. They got the results back on the lab tests of that envelope you got in New York. Not surprisingly, there were no fingerprints."

All at once, Jessica found she had to sit down again. Blindly she made her way back to the chair and felt around for the seat, asking weakly, "And the blood?"

"Was from a squirrel."

Jessica shut her eyes, feeling the bile rise in her throat. What perverse mind would destroy an animal for a cheap thrill? "Why would someone want to do that?" she whispered.

Mark shrugged diffidently, still watching her face. "To scare you. Or maybe to make you forget something they think you know."

Jessica looked up at him sharply. It didn't take a genius to figure out he too suspected she was withholding evidence. *Damn him* for being able to read her emotions so easily.

Before she could question him further, the police cars pulled up out front and doors slammed. Seconds later, two uniformed officers walked into her house. "Ms. Lowell?"

Jessica nodded briefly. She led them into the living room and explained what she'd found.

Mark introduced himself, saying only that he was a friend who'd dropped by moments after she got home.

"And you didn't see anything or hear anyone?" the policeman asked Jessica.

She shook her head. "I guess they'd already left by the time I got here." She was thankful for that, and yet wasn't. She wanted to know who was behind this. "Except for the phone and front door, we haven't touched anything," Mark said.

"Any idea what they were looking for?" the policeman inquired.

Suzette's book. Jessica shook her head once more, avoiding Mark's penetrating gaze. "No, I don't."

She watched as they walked around, one making notes on the damage, another dusting for prints.

"We'll need you to tell us if anything is missing," the policeman said.

Jessica nodded, and began her own investigation.

Unfortunately, the burglar had taken something, she realized moments later as she sorted through the rubble that had been the contents of her desk. Several old letters from Suzette were missing. She recalled with relief that none had mentioned the book she'd been working on. They'd been mostly news about old college friends, talk of clothes and vacation plans. Happily, the burglar hadn't gotten the one she'd received the day before in the doctored Publishers' Clearing House envelope. That letter was still in Jessica's purse and would not leave her. The envelope was also a good disguise, as few people had any interest in what many considered junk mail.

"Everything okay?" Mark came up to stand beside her.

Jessica nodded, again avoiding his eyes.

"You're sure nothing was missing?" he pressed again. He certainly seemed to think she was hiding something, she reflected wryly.

"Positive." Jessica strode to the front door, where the police officers were examining the lock. "Well, no damage here. None to the back door or windows, either," one of them said.

"Which means what?" Jessica asked nervously.

"That either the thief was a professional and knew how to pick a lock without doing damage, or he had a key."

"Seems unlikely it was a routine burglary, since the television and the stereo weren't taken," Mark interjected.

The policeman continued. "Does anyone have access to your house, Ms. Lowell? A milkman, or maid service? Do you routinely leave a key outside the door somewhere, hidden under the welcome mat or—?"

"I've got one hidden under a planter on the back porch."

"Want to check and see if it's still there?" the cop asked.

Looking distraught, Jessica raced to the back door. The key was exactly where she'd left it.

"Does anyone know you keep a key hidden there?" the policeman asked.

"No. I'm very careful about that."

"It'd be better not to leave one outside at all," Mark cut in.

The policeman agreed. "The key's got several overlapping smudged prints on it—nothing we can use for a positive ID."

"The fingerprints are probably mine, anyway," Jessica murmured, wishing she knew who had done this as they walked back into her house.

"So who else has a key to your house?" the policeman resumed his questioning.

"No one," Jessica said, "except—"

"Me." A voice spoke from behind them. Everyone turned, to see Bennett walking up the path. He looked at her worriedly. "What's going on, Jessica?"

Briefly she explained what she'd found when she returned home. "Bennett has a key," she told the officers.

"She's got one to my place, too," Bennett said casually, not elaborating.

"We check each other's places when we're out of town," Jessica explained, not wanting anyone to get the wrong idea.

Mark Gallagher was still watching Bennett carefully.

"What about Suzette? Didn't she have a key?" Bennett asked.

Jessica nodded. "Yes, she did."

"Where's that key now?" the policeman asked.

"The Washington police confiscated her purse and keys. They're supposed to send them to me when their paperwork is completed, but I haven't received them yet."

Jessica's explanation tapered off as she noticed the tension around her. Mark was staring at Bennett almost angrily. Did he suspect Bennett of the break-in? Jessica didn't want to think her old friend capable of such treachery, but admitted to herself that the thought had crossed her mind—albeit reluctantly. Then again, almost anyone could have found the key hidden under the planter on her back porch, used it and simply put it back. If they'd been wearing gloves and hadn't been seen, no one would ever know....

The police officers were baffled by the half explanations. Graciously Bennett explained about Suzette's unfortunate demise, and the strain it had put on all of them. He looked at Mark angrily, his jealousy showing as he commented, "Though what Gallagher is doing here now, I don't know."

"Same as you," Mark said evenly, holding Bennett's gaze unflinchingly. "I'm looking after Jessica's interests."

Jessica didn't think she needed anyone looking after her interests half as much as she needed to know where the rest of Suzette's book and her journal were.

"We'll run the prints through the lab. In the meantime I think you should have the locks changed. And if you have insurance, you'll want to contact your agent before you clean up."

"I will. Thank you."

"Jessica, I think you ought to come and stay with me, at least until you get things back to normal," Bennett said, as soon as the policemen had left.

Mark looked at her. She knew he was thinking that she and Bennett had been lovers. Ignoring him, she turned back to Bennett.

"Thank you for the offer, Bennett, but I think I'll just check into a motel." She knew she wouldn't feel safe in her home that night, violated as it had been. Only time and cleaning up would wash away the bitter feelings that were brewing in her right now.

Bennett's eyes grew pleading. "You know that's not necessary. I'd be glad to put you up."

"I know, but I'd rather be alone."

Bennett glared at Mark, as if Jessica's refusal were all his fault. "Don't you think it's about time you left?" he suggested curtly.

Mark looked at Jessica, then nodded slowly. "I'll be in touch," he promised.

"What did he mean by that?" Bennett demanded when the door had closed behind him.

"I've no idea," Jessica said, watching Mark depart. She wished she did. She wished she weren't so aware of him.

Bennett stayed until the locksmith came and secured the locks, and Jessica had notified her insurance agent, who promised to come over first thing in the morning to help her fill out the claim forms.

Exhausted and drained, she drove to the closest motel. No sooner had she checked in than she heard a rap at her door.

She opened the door a crack, leaving on the security chain. Mark Gallagher was standing outside, looking handsome and indomitable in the yellow neon light. "I just thought I'd tell you I'm staying here, too, in the next room. Yell if you need anything."

Jessica was stunned. How had he managed that? His sudden appearances just had to be questioned, but she was too exhausted to do so right now. She quickly undressed and climbed into bed after double-checking the sturdy front door bolt.

An hour later, she was still tossing and turning. Getting up, she retrieved Suzette's letter from her purse. Over and over she focused on the words Suzette had chosen. *They must have special meaning. But what?* She'd gone literally everywhere they had roomed together, looked up their old hiding place. And except for that "resort summer" they'd spent at Indian Lake...

Indian Lake! Why hadn't she remembered sooner?

IT WAS SHORTLY AFTER DAWN when Jessica crept out of her room, suitcase in hand. No sooner had she opened her car door than Mark was outside, too. "A little early to be going to work, isn't it?" he said, strolling casually toward her.

She tossed her suitcase into the back. "I'm behind."

"How about having breakfast with me?" Despite his know-it-all grin, his tone was cordial.

"Uh, thanks, but no thanks," Jessica said, getting in behind the wheel. "I'm in a hurry."

He held on to the car door, deliberately delaying her exit. "You've got to eat, especially if you plan to work all day. Unless there's a special reason you're in such a hurry."

It was all Jessica could do not to grab the car door out of his hands and race out of the parking lot. But she knew such a scene would only draw more attention to herself. He'd simply get into his car and follow her. *No.* She had to get rid of him using logic this time, make him think she really wasn't onto or up to anything, a task that wasn't going to be easy when he was still baiting her so deliberately. He'd been tailing since last night—and before that—to find out what she was up to. She swallowed hard and answered airily, "No special reason. Just lots of work to do."

"Let me buy you breakfast then. I insist." His attitude was properly gallant.

Under the circumstances, Jessica was unable to appreciate his effort at courtliness. "Well, that's awfully kind of you," she drawled, unable to keep the smugness completely out of her voice, "but the coffee shop doesn't open for another half hour yet."

Unperturbed, he shoved both hands into the pockets of his leather bomber jacket. "No problem," he countered easily, like a poker player who'd just revealed a full house. "There's a twenty-four-hour truck stop down the road."

Jessica smiled sweetly. Maybe that would be the best place to dump him. And he was right. She did have to eat; it was going to be a very long day. "Okay." She smiled with false congeniality. "Get in."

He's harmless, she told herself as she drove. *Nosy but harmless.*

Mark didn't speak until they were seated in a booth at the truck stop. Steam clouded the windows, and the red vinyl upholstery was cracked, but the air was thick with the smells of freshly baked biscuits and hot coffee.

"You're annoyed with me, aren't you?" he asked, as soon as they'd placed their order.

Very annoyed, she thought. "What makes you think that?" Jessica asked civilly.

"The look on your face. You can't quite make that smile of yours seem genuine."

Damn him for pointing that out. "It's early, okay?"

He nodded sagely, spreading his napkin on his lap. "And you're up to something. Call it the news hound in me, but I'd like to know what."

She noticed he hadn't forgotten his camera. He lugged that neatly-encased equipment with the same devotion she applied to lugging the manuscript around with her. "So you can take some more pictures?"

"Maybe. And maybe my curiosity has to do with the fact that I knew Suzette. And I don't like the cover-up going on in DC. Let's be honest with each other, okay? I don't buy the suicide theory, and neither do you. So what do you say we start working together? You level with me, I'll level with you. Maybe together we can figure this thing out.''

In a sense his offer was tempting, because she was tired of going it alone. On the other hand, she'd watched Mark snapping photos the day of Suzette's funeral, and seen for herself the hardened curiosity in him that mirrored the same quality in other veteran news hounds and photojournalists. Added to that, her gut feeling was that Mark Gallagher hadn't told her the entire truth yet. He was like a barracuda, always after her. . . .

Besides, she reasoned further, if he knew about the book Suzette had been working on, he'd want it for *Personalities*. And that could totally ruin, or at least dilute the results of whatever it was Suzette had been investigating.

For Suzette's sake she had to go this alone until she knew better what she was dealing with.

''What are your plans for the rest of the day?'' he asked, once their bacon and eggs had been delivered.

Jessica was so shocked that she almost choked on her orange juice. ''What do you mean—?'' *Damn*. He'd caught her off guard.

''That phone call you made about an hour ago to the paper, saying you wouldn't be in today and you'd explain later,'' he prompted her memory dryly.

She felt her face grow warm. Her fork was motionless in her hand. ''How did you know about that?''

He smiled at her complacently, signaling he wasn't about to let her get away with a thing, not now, not ever. ''The walls at the motel were paper-thin. When I heard you up and around after five, I made it my business to hear everything possible.''

''Glass against the wall?'' She ground out the question, enraged.

"Hey, it works."

"Scum!"

He bared his teeth in a determined smile. "So where are you going?"

None of your business. She made an airy gesture. "To see an old college roommate, who hasn't heard about Suzette's death."

"Then why did you lie about it to your boss at the paper?"

He had too many questions, and she was fast running out of answers. "Would you excuse me?" she asked coldly and headed toward the ladies' room.

Once in there, she splashed some water onto her face and willed her hands to stop their trembling. *Okay, first things first. She had to ditch Mark Gallagher. But how? No way was he going to simply let her run out of there, not without a struggle. Unless . . .*

With an idea forming in her mind, she walked back to the table. Several truckers with burly tattoos on their forearms looked up to watch. They looked grumpy and tired and every bit as invincible as Mark. *Okay. Maybe she wasn't a match for him, physically anyway, but they were.*

"You feeling okay?" Mark asked, watching her with narrowed eyes.

"No, I'm not okay," Jessica said, loudly enough for the truckers to hear. "How can you even expect me to be, after the—the night we just spent together in that sleazy motel!" She glared at him fiercely, drawing on the genuine resentment she felt toward him. To her satisfaction, his face began to grow red. "How could you do that to me?" she screamed shrilly, throwing up her arms as if in disgust before flinging them back to her sides. "And then—then to offer me breakfast—" she blurted out even louder ''—as some sort of payment, as if that would make up for what you tried to do, when you know how I've been feeling of late—'' Ending her tirade with a dramatic sob and a wail of dismay, she put both hands over her face.

Mark got to his feet, a look of real confusion, growing anger and humiliation on his face. ''What the—?''

She moved as if to step past him. As she'd predicted, he moved to block her path. Help wasn't long in coming.

''Trouble, miss?'' One of the burly truckers was suddenly at her side.

She turned to him, tears of real frustration in her eyes. ''I just want him to leave me alone,'' she whispered harshly. ''Please make him leave me alone!''

The trucker took in her tears and turned back to Mark. One beefy hand around Mark's arm, he said, ''You heard her, buddy. *Back off.*''

''Wait—'' Mark said, clearly not wanting to fight.

Jessica used the opportunity to scoot past. ''Thanks. Thanks a million,'' she whispered, already breaking into a run.

Behind her she heard the crash of broken dishes, the sound of men scuffling, then someone hitting the floor. She didn't pause to look back. She just ran, and kept right on running.

FIVE HUNDRED miles away, Vinnie Forsythe approached the Cadillac. The driver reached over to let him in.

For several seconds they sat in tense silence. ''What do you want?'' the driver asked.

''Money. Pure and simple.'' What Vinnie always wanted.

"Why should I pay you?" his well-heeled victim spat out.

Vinnie sneered slyly. "Because I know about Suzette Howar. I have a good idea of what she was on to, and enough information to make the investigation into her death the hottest bit of news this city has ever seen."

Silence. "What do I have to do with Ms. Howar?" the driver asked, staring unseeingly ahead.

Vinnie could see his target was nervous. Beads of sweat were rolling down his quarry's forehead, onto the silk scarf wrapped around the man's neck. He hoped the quarry wasn't going to try anything violent, because just to be on the safe side he'd brought both his knife and his gun. His fingers circled the cold metal in his pocket. He had no compunction about killing, none at all.

"I don't have a lot of time," Vinnie said impatiently. "If you're going to pay me, say so. If not..." He let his voice trail off. There were other fish in the sea.

The other man's mouth trembled. "I have your word of honor you won't say a word?"

Lord, what a sap! "Cross my heart," Vinnie promised sincerely, making the appropriate sign.

The quarry stared at him with utter loathing, then reached forward and picked up the fine leather satchel off the floor. Vinnie put out a staying hand. In the other he held the gun. "Allow me," he said, with a sleazy smile.

There was money inside, all right, he noted seconds later. Lots of it.

Just that swiftly he felt a sharp pinprick in midthigh. He gasped, and dropping the gun reflexively, tried to pull the needle free. *Too late.* The drug was already taking effect.

Two seconds later he was unconscious.

The quarry smiled, watching as Vinnie slumped into the seat. Greed made people so careless. Street drugs were so effective, especially when administered at a lethal dosage.

Getting out of the car, the quarry searched quickly for spies. There were none, but it was almost dawn. He would have to work quickly. Taking Vinnie from the car, he dragged the small man's body to a deserted stand of trees. Putting him up against the side of a tree, he placed Vinnie's hand around the gun, the barrel against Vinnie's head, his finger on the trigger.

Thanks to the silencer Vinnie'd already placed on his weapon, the sound was barely audible.

Vinnie slumped over, blood streaming from his head.

The quarry smiled. *So easy. So clean.*

Vinnie'd been a fool to act against his adversary. So had Suzette. But the quarry had had the last laugh. And now it was over, all over. The work could go on. And on. And on.

Chapter Nine

Jessica arrived at Indian Lake shortly after noon. To her delight, the retired teacher who owned the cabins was at home, watching her favorite soap opera. Jessica wasn't sure Mrs. Webster would remember her, but as it turned out she had nothing to worry about on that score.

"Of course I remember you, Jessica Lowell! You worked here four summers ago."

"Right. In the family-style restaurant across the lake," Jessica said, stepping inside the cozy parlor.

"You and your girlfriend Suzette stayed here. You helped me clean the cabins every Saturday afternoon, and in exchange I gave you a reduced rent on the cabin."

Jessica smiled back reminiscingly. "That was a great summer." In their spare time they'd hiked in the woods, fished and swum in the lake.

"Your friend Suzette was here not too long ago, too," Mrs. Webster continued, sitting back in her rocker. "Thanksgiving, I think it was. The cabins are closed for the winter now, but she convinced me to rent her one for the weekend for old times' sake, and of course I did. Didn't see much of her though. She kept pretty much to herself—working on some papers, she was."

And Jessica hadn't even known Suzette was in Ohio.

She took a deep breath, bracing herself for the lies she knew she had to tell. "That's why I'm here, Mrs. Webster. You see Suzette mentioned to me she thought she might have left some of her belongings here. I told her I'd check it out first chance I got."

Mrs. Webster's brow furrowed. "Hmm. I guess that's possible. I really haven't been down there, since Suzette insisted upon cleaning the cabin herself before she left. But you're welcome to take a look if you like." Pushing herself out of her chair, she walked over to get the key out of the rolltop desk. "You know the way to cabin eight, don't you?"

"Yes, ma'am. And thank you." Jessica paused at the door. "You wouldn't mind if I . . . well, if I kind of took my time looking around, would you? I—this is bringing back a lot of memories for me—"

"You girls always were sentimental. Sure, take your time."

Jessica walked briskly down the path and through a thick stand of trees to cabin eight. She was so excited that her hands were shaking.

Inside, the cabin was smaller than she remembered. It had a living room furnished with a vinyl sofa and braided rug, a kitchen with a wood-burning stove, a bath that was primitive at best, and a bedroom with two army surplus cots. The cabin was as cold inside as it was outside, and Jessica's teeth were chattering as she put her purse down and started to look around.

Where would Suzette have hidden the journal? she wondered. Was the rest of the manuscript here, as well?

Deciding she needed to be methodical in her search, Jessica started with the closet, moved to the mattresses, the sofa cushions, then to the spaces underneath the furniture. She even looked in the refrigerator, to no avail. She was about to give up when she remembered the decorative milk jug on the porch. She peered into the jug's deep well, holding her breath, then expelled it slowly; disappointment washed over her. It wasn't there, either. Going slowly back inside, she cast another slow look around, realizing she'd searched everywhere but inside the wood stove.

No, she thought. Suzette wouldn't—

Or would she?

Opening up the stove, she found nothing. Then, just before giving up, she touched the handle of the broiler under the oven. Sliding it out gingerly, almost reverently, her breath held to the bursting point, she peered inside. Nothing lay atop the gray metal tray, yet on a hunch, feeling she was getting closer, she lifted it—and gasped. There lay a familiar object in its dark leather binding: Suzette's journal.

THE JOURNAL tucked safely into the large pocket of her winter coat, Jessica drove back to Spring Valley. No sooner had she gotten out of her car than Mark Gallagher stepped out of his motel room.

"What you did to me back there was lousy," he said quietly, remaining a good distance away, his hands tucked indolently in the pockets of his trousers, one shoulder jammed lazily against the door to his room. He had taken a beating. She could see a cut on his lip and another just below one eye. Jessica's heart was pounding. It wasn't her fault he wouldn't leave her alone, she thought, defiantly pushing the feeling of guilt away. "So was following me," she retorted icily.

"In other words, it serves me right," he muttered sarcastically, arching his brows, "for trying to protect you?"

Protect her! Was that what he called it? "From whom and from what?" she demanded aggravatedly, stepping toward him.

"That's just it. Right now we don't know who broke into your apartment or killed your friend."

She ignored his statement, focusing on the plural pronoun. "We?" Who was he working with? Suddenly it didn't seem as though he was referring to the people at the magazine at all.

A muscle twitched in his jaw; he was obviously furious with himself for that slip.

And suddenly she knew he was hiding much too much. "How'd you get back here?"

"I hitched a ride with a trucker."

"And then waited for me."

"Yes."

"Why?"

He was silent, debating with himself. His eyes grew forbidding. "I can't explain."

Fine. "Then I can't stay here with you." She whirled and started for her car. He caught her arm, his grip not hurting her, but not something she could easily break, either. He pulled her around to face him so that they were standing toe-to-toe, so close that she could feel his body heat and sense the strength in his sinewy frame. For long moments they stared at one another, then he sighed heavily as if making some sort of decision, and reached for a black leather wallet that contained a photo identification badge. The insignia was bold and to the point. "CIA!" she exclaimed.

His answering look was droll and long-suffering, as if this was the last place in the world he wanted to be. As quickly as he'd showed her his badge, he put it away. Releasing her, he again assumed his lazy stance against his motel room door, his jacket hanging open to reveal a soft azure-blue sweater. "Suffice it to say we think you're in danger," he said quietly.

Aware her pulse was racing and that she was achingly aware of him, Jessica took several steps back. "How do I know that badge is real?"

He nodded laconically toward the interior of the motel and spoke in a low voice. "Call the agency."

Jessica stared at him warily. "I don't have the number."

"Information will give it to you. When you get through, tell them who you are and ask for this man." He handed her a note. On it was scrawled the name Noah Case. Mark had apparently anticipated this scene between them. Noticing her baffled air, he continued. "He's my boss. He'll confirm my identity. Until then I'll be in my room. You can come over when you're ready to talk." He slipped inside.

Jessica stared after him, stunned, then quickly went inside and made the call. The conversation was almost over before it started. Crisp, efficient operators immediately put her through to Noah Case's office. Brusquely he answered her questions until the end, when an apologetic tone entered his harsh voice. "I'm sorry things came to this. Mark thought they might. My suggestion to you, for your own and for your dead friend's sake, is to cooperate."

Still feeling a little shell-shocked, Jessica went to Mark's room and knocked on the door. He ushered her inside. She noted immediately his bags were already packed; since hers were in the trunk of her car, she supposed they were ready to go.

"I take it he confirmed my identity to your satisfaction?" he asked dryly.

Her throat tight, she nodded. "And then some."
She'd also had Noah's assistant describe him, down to
the color of his eyes.

Staring at him, Jessica sighed. "Suzette's death really
was no accident, was it?" And the CIA knew it, too.
"You think she was murdered." Jessica felt a flood of
relief, followed by a new surge of puzzlement. "But
why?"

He shrugged. "Right now we're as much in the dark
as you. Because she worked for Rothschild, Suzette was
often privy to highly confidential information. He's on
the Senate Defense Committee, and collectively they're
not known for their ability to keep a secret. For all we
know, she could've been milking the senator for information, then selling it to outsiders or political rivals."

"Now that's a lie! Suzette was not involved in es-
pionage."

Mark arched his brows in disagreement. "Someone
sure wanted her dead. To this point, we haven't come up
with any other reason."

Except the manuscript, Jessica thought, *that they still
know nothing about.*

"Besides, everything about her death smacks of a
professional hit. She was already running scared, book-
ing herself on a flight out of DC, not showing up for
work that day. And then you arrived and get assaulted.
Ten to one something was going down that night."

"You think her murderer wanted me dead, too?"

"If that were the case, then you would be dead."
Mark sat down on the edge of the bed and gestured for
her to take the chair closest to the door. "No. I think he
or she just wanted you scared, confused."

She'd been that, all right. "Do you have any idea who
did it?"

"Our guess is, whoever did it is someone Suzette knew or felt fairly comfortable with, because there was no sign of forced entry to her apartment. No signs of bruises on her body or of a struggle."

"So she let them in?"

"Either that, or they had a key and were able to come up behind her and surprise her."

Jessica told him about Suzette's phone call to her the night she was killed. "She was frightened."

"But obviously the murderer hadn't shown up yet," Mark mused, intrigued.

"No, I guess not."

Mark was silent. He ran a hand through his hair. "Look, I know you don't have to cooperate with us. But I need your help. Would you consider working with me, instead of avoiding me?"

Suddenly it didn't seem such a bad option. It was better than working alone in the dark. "I'd do anything to see Suzette's murderer brought to justice."

"So would I."

The matter settled, Mark was all business. "Okay, the first thing we have to do is get you checked out of this motel." He glanced at his watch impatiently. "If we hurry, we'll still have time to catch a plane back to Washington."

She stared at him in bewilderment, aware he was already moving very fast. "We?" she croaked. She'd expected to cooperate with him, maybe even show him the journal, but this . . .

"You're going with me." He seemed to take it for granted she would.

But her life wasn't that simple. "Wait a minute. My job with the paper—"

"Take a leave of absence. Tell them you're too distraught to work. If they say no, forget them."

"Easy for you to say."

He met her eyes levelly and pointed out calmly, "It's the only way you'll be safe."

"If I'm with you." Her tone sounded oddly breathless as she stood up.

"Yeah. And maybe not even then, considering what happened last night." Slowly he got to his feet. "There's no doubt in my mind someone wants you to stop your snooping. The envelope at the airport, the break-in—they all add up to warnings to back off."

"But I'm not going to back off," Jessica said, thrusting her chin out stubbornly.

"I know that, too." Something akin to respect glimmered in his light green eyes.

She had no doubt he could protect them if it came to a showdown. "All right," she said finally, her decision made. It would be a relief not to have to shoulder this inquiry alone, to have someone else pondering the inconsistencies, too.

Two hours later, she and Mark were on a plane back to Washington. The only seats available were in first class. As she stretched her legs wearily in front of her, Jessica was glad of the extra room.

"I can't believe I left my house in that condition," she murmured. Luckily, her boss at the paper had agreed to give her a few extra days off to get Suzette's affairs settled, since there was no one else to do so. But three or four more days was all the time she had—they couldn't afford to be without her any longer, Jessica knew.

"I'll go back with you, first chance we get, and help you set things to rights," Mark said. She saw from the look in his eyes that he really did want to help her. Again she felt that sense of relief at the knowledge she was no longer completely alone in this quest of hers. Maybe she should trust him, after all. Maybe someone else should know about the journal... and the novel Suzette had been writing.

"And what are we going to do in the meantime?"

"Try and get close enough to the senator to find out what Suzette must have known or been up to."

The plan sounded almost too simple for it to work. "Senator Rothschild's very protective of his staff. He takes a highly personal interest in everyone who works for him. He won't talk to you—at least not in any real depth."

"Yeah, but his wife might. Gloria's been known to have quite a loose tongue—never more so than when she's had a few."

"You're planning to take advantage of her when her defenses are down?" Somehow that seemed wrong. But it had also been wrong for Suzette to be murdered, Jessica thought, already rationalizing whatever she would have to do to bring Suzette's murderer to justice.

"No, I wouldn't do that to anyone with a drinking problem. But if we just happen to be there—" His voice trailed off speculatively. He would make full use of any opportunity that presented itself.

She took a good look at him, aware he had never looked more ruggedly handsome than he did at that moment. "You already have an idea on how to do that, don't you?" She tried to quell her racing pulse.

He nodded. "Starting tomorrow, I'm going to begin a collection of comprehensive in-depth profiles and photo essays on political wives. Of course, I'll need a writing partner on this."

"You're asking me to help?"

He nodded again. "I need to keep you near me, to make sure you're safe. I don't like what's been happening to you of late. Also, it would help if you could listen to whatever is being said, in case anything ties in with what you already know."

She would do it for Suzette, Jessica determined grimly. "And when we're finished—?"

"We'll publish the article, either as a series in a magazine or maybe even in book form, depending on how successful it is."

She knew he had the reputation professionally from his work at *Personalities* to make it all happen.

Jessica was quiet for a while. She wanted to read the journal so badly that she could hardly stand it, but she was reluctant to do so while they were sitting on the plane.

"What hotel am I staying in?" she asked, glancing idly out the window at the black night below. She knew she would have to tell Mark everything she knew eventually, but it would have to be later, when they were alone, when there was no chance they'd be overheard.

"You're not."

She looked up, stunned. "You're staying with me," he said pragmatically. "It'll be safer."

Chapter Ten

"Wait a minute! I can't—"

"Sure you can. Besides, it's the only way our sudden partnership will make sense to outsiders. Unless you're worried about what your boyfriend will think," Mark finished dryly, a gleam in his eyes.

"Bennett's not my boyfriend," she answered hotly, then lowering her voice added defensively, "He's just a friend. What—what makes you think—?"

Mark shrugged and looked away from her. "The way he hovers over you whenever possible. His jealous re-action to my presence in your home last night." He turned back to Jessica, his expression hard and faintly accusing. "*He* thinks there's something between you and him."

"I know." Jessica was quiet. "I've never tried to lead him on, but—"

"There was a time when you were close?" Mark asked softly, his attitude changing to one of compassion.

She nodded. "When my mother died. She was ill a long time." She explained briefly.

Mark studied her curiously. "Is that why you never went to New York to begin your career? I've read your stuff. You're an excellent writer. Too excellent to be stuck only reporting on the happenings at the local 4-H club.''

Jessica knew and part of her agreed. The other half, the saner half, thought it too risky to venture to New York on the hope of a successful writing career. ''I like life in a small town.''

Again he had that mischievous gleam in his eyes. ''You're telling me you don't ever lust after the excitement of big-city life?''

She had been restless lately. Very restless. But she sensed it would be a mistake to tell Mark Gallagher that. Not when he seemed to have a solution, a plan for her every question and calamity.

''I like the way my life is now,'' she said as the Fasten Seat Belts sign came on.

Mark made a vaguely dissenting sound and glanced out the window as the lights of National Airport came into view. ''Looks like we'll be landing soon.''

Jessica sighed. It was time for their act to begin.

''RELAX, we'll be safe here,'' Mark assured as he carried their bags into the hotel suite.

She wasn't worried about burglars. She was worried about Mark. *He* might be used to such casual living arrangements, but she wasn't. ''There's only one bedroom.'' *With one double bed.*

''So we'll flip for it, and take turns sleeping on the couch.''

''That sounds fair.'' She didn't fear him, only what he did to her pulse whenever she was near him.

''Relax, I'm not going to ravish you.''

Her mouth curved wryly. ''That's a relief.''

''Yeah, well, don't get too relieved,'' he remarked in jest. ''You'll bruise my ego.''

She slipped off her coat, but kept a firm grip on her purse, as Suzette's journal was inside.

"You can put your purse down now," Mark said dryly. "I promise I won't bother it."

She knew he had noticed the stranglehold she'd kept on her purse during their entire journey, but had also been relieved when he hadn't pressed her to explain. She needed to soak in the information he'd revealed about himself; allow some trust to grow between them. Now she knew it was time she told him everything.

As briefly as possible, she explained about the book Suzette had been working on, the note in the Publishers' Clearing House contest envelope, the first hundred pages she'd received via registered mail, the journal she'd located at the cabin but had not yet been able to sit down and read.

"And you think that was why she was killed?" Mark asked.

"Yes," Jessica nodded bleakly, "but other than myself, as far as I know, no one but her literary agent Tamara North is aware she was writing it."

"That's why you went to New York last week," Mark ascertained slowly.

"Yes. I had to find out what was going on. I never knew the agent's name, just that Suzette had one. Then when I was in Suzette's apartment I found the agent's name and address on an empty business envelope." She paused. "Were you following me that day—to Tamara's office?"

Slowly he nodded. "We knew from the beginning you were our most valuable—hell, our only—lead." His voice deepened roughly. "I also didn't want to see you get hurt."

"You didn't know me."

His eyes held hers honestly. "I knew enough," he said simply, letting his emotions show for the first time in quite a while.

Silence stretched between them, this time pleasurably, giving Jessica an odd thrill. She knew it was dangerous to let herself even consider the idea of getting involved with a man like Mark—a man who seemed to have few ties—but there was no denying the simmering attraction between them, and it went deeper than just the physical. Somehow it was both emotional and mental, as if in him she had finally met her match, the man who would challenge and provoke and get the best out of her, whether she wanted to respond or not.

She realized abruptly that she'd been staring. She forced herself to shake off the ludicrously romantic thoughts. *It must be the situation,* she thought, *the unreality of it all.*

He was still watching her, kindly now. "Will you let me read the first one hundred pages of Suzette's novel? Her journal?"

Jessica nodded.

The suite was quiet as Jessica settled down to read the journal, Mark the first pages of "Dreams of Glory." The journal had been started the week Suzette had moved to Washington to work for the senator. The entries were sporadic, dealing at first with trivial details like her new apartment, Audrey's jealousy of her, the office back-stabbing that was done almost as routinely as the filing. Entries dated six months later were more disturbing. Suzette agonized over whether she should see a psychiatrist—was she crazy to think that everyone else was crazy?—that a mysterious conspiracy was going on right on Capitol Hill and no one had noticed the strange goings-on or the malevolent pattern beginning to emerge? And she wondered, if she did go to see a psychiatrist, whether it would be considered a weakness. Then, once she had taken the step and contacted Dr. Conti she was glad she had. After all, there was no shame in seeing a psychiatrist. Plenty of people under stress had done the same, and Conti had a reputation, among the upper classes especially, for being the kind of man you could really trust to keep a confidence. After having been to see him a few times, Suzette knew that was true and even talked to him openly about her anxiety over her book. Was she taking on too much? Or was hers a normal writer's anxiety? Conti had believed the latter. And eventually so had Suzette, although it had taken several sessions and much fatherly reassurance for them to achieve that.

Jessica stopped and read several passages aloud to Mark. "Suzette? In need of a father figure?" Mark was as stunned as Jessica.

"I know," Jessica murmured. "She always seemed so fiercely independent. But maybe her turning to Conti isn't so strange. I mean, she never had much of a relationship with her own father. He was a cold, rigid man. He died when she was in her teens."

"And her mother?"

"She had a stroke and died a couple of years later. I remember Suzette finished college on her insurance money and moved to DC on what little she had left. I was all she had." And it was up to Jessica to make sense of her death.

They went back to their reading. The next journal entry was dated several weeks later, in early fall. Suzette wrote that the sessions with Dr. Conti were still helping her enormously—sometimes she couldn't believe how good she felt about herself when she left his office—but in between times she still felt pressured about completing the work on her book. She'd started out wanting to write fiction, but as she got deeper into the project, she felt nonfiction might better suit her topic. Yet she was also worried about being sued for libel, so she decided finally to go back to fiction and work up her material into a thinly disguised kiss and tell novel.

Long minutes later, Mark had finished reading the manuscript. Jessica summarized for him the early entries in the diary, which he planned to read later, then showed him the last few entries in the journal, all dated the previous October. Over and over again, Suzette had hinted at something vaguely nefarious going on that only she seemed able to see. She wasn't sure where the activity was taking place, but thought she'd overheard some talk of a gloriously restful mansion in the country that several wives had been using as a retreat. She'd been unable to discover either where it was located or whom it belonged to. All she knew was that the wives were running to some specific place every time the burden of being in the public eye grew too heavy, and that the whole business was a closely guarded secret.

The next entry was dated three weeks later. It didn't make a whole lot of sense to Jessica, appearing to be just isolated ramblings about the upper echelon of the DC wives. Suzette had written that "some in the group seem bizarre, strangely confused…the ones with families seem the most firmly grounded in reality, but they are also in some instances the most troubled."

Jessica read that again. "What do you suppose that means?"

Interested, he sat down beside her, stretching his long legs in front of him. "I don't know. She was looking for some sort of pattern. Do you think that's true?"

Jessica thought of all the people she'd met and interviewed over the past four years in her work on the paper. "Sometimes women with children do seem to have it more together—maybe because their focus is not solely on themselves but on their children's welfare, too. But they also have bigger problems, maybe because they have more people to worry about and care for. So I guess they simultaneously have it easier in some respects and harder in others."

"It's the same for guys—at least the ones I know with kids." He spoke as if those were few.

Curious, Jessica asked, "Do most of your co-workers have families?" Idly she wondered what it would be like to be married to someone who worked for the CIA.

"No. The agency doesn't want field agents who could be blackmailed, and anyone with a family is always very vulnerable on that level. As far as the agency goes, the fewer ties an operative has, the better."

It made sense. "That doesn't bother you?"

He shrugged. "So far I've never wanted to settle down."

And a rolling stone gathers no moss, she thought.

"You look like you don't approve," he commented quietly.

He'd read her expression accurately, she realized, and dug her toe into the carpet. "It just sounds like a lonely way to live."

He was suddenly very still as he regarded her thoughtfully. "You're lonely, too, aren't you?"

But with a difference, she thought. "Not by choice," she said quietly. Most times she wished she had a family, a husband, children. She wanted to be surrounded by people who loved her, people she loved. Instead, her circle of close friends and loved ones was narrowing precariously. First her mother had died, then Suzette, and now she and Bennett were becoming estranged.

But dwelling on such problems wouldn't help, not at the moment, anyway. Depression hit her anew as Jessica forced herself to read on. "It says here some of the senate wives were privately battling substance abuse or neurotic behavior." Suzette had begun to see a pattern emerging, which had then made her wonder if she wasn't the one who was getting a little neurotic. In the margin she'd written her doubts, wondering if maybe she'd concentrated too much of her research on a single area and was missing the overall picture.

"Hey," Mark said, as they turned the page. "Here's a list of the political wives she'd been surreptitiously zeroing in on."

"Pamela Fieldler, Gloria Rothschild . . ."

"Along with about thirty others," Mark observed. And it was there the entries stopped.

He looked at Jessica, his expression perplexed. "I wonder what it all means?"

"I don't know," Jessica said. But she was scared again, and she didn't like it.

"WE'RE ALL SO EXCITED about your new project," Pamela Fieldler said the following morning. She was perfectly coiffed and attired, looking as if she had the world on a string.

"Thanks for letting us come to your luncheon today." Mark sent her an easy grin. He had called that morning, trumpeting his intention to write an in-depth study of prominent Washington wives.

"Well, what better place to announce your intention to do the interviews?" Pamela took them around, introducing them to the wives gathered together. The reactions to their presence were varied, but had one thing in common; everyone there seemed to respect the power of the press and the journalist's capacity to make or break someone's career, either through the printed word or photo opportunity.

Jessica hung back slightly, muttering to Mark in a private aside, "If there's a link between all these women and what Suzette was working on, I don't see it."

"Patience, darling, patience," Mark murmured back. "Rome wasn't built in a day, and neither was any good investigation."

"Shall we get started?" Pamela asked, after everyone had left. She had volunteered to be the first to be interviewed, and they had decided to begin immediately after her luncheon was over.

While Mark moved about, taking pictures of Pamela from every angle, Jessica began asking questions. "How did you and the senator meet?"

"I was a dancer, working in the chorus line on a Broadway play. He came backstage to tell me how much he admired my performance, and the rest was history." They had courted, married and in rapid succession had three children, all of whom were now in college and doing very well.

"Do you ever wish you had stuck with the dancing or continued with it in some fashion, maybe opened your own studio or gotten into choreography?" Jessica asked.

"All the time. But life was different then." She went on to explain why she had quit her work as a dancer as soon as she married. "Twenty years ago, a woman was expected to subordinate her own wishes to those of her husband."

"It's not that way anymore."

"No, it isn't. And I thank God for that." Regret laced her voice.

"There was no way you could go back to it?" Jessica suggested. She hated to see any talent go unused.

Pamela shrugged. "Maybe, if I hadn't ruined my knee. I was in a car accident after the birth of my first child. Several tendons were severed. The damage was repaired surgically, but I no longer have the range of motion or flexibility I once did in that leg. I have to be careful not to reinjure it, and there are still many things I can't do—run up and down stairs, for instance. I can do a few exercises, however, to strengthen the joint—swimming, for instance. You needn't feel sorry for me, my dear." She accepted Jessica's sympathy with a smile. "Life goes on. And I do too."

"You're one of the most outspoken of the senate wives," Jessica remarked, taking a new tack.

"I've always believed in saying what was on my mind."

"That doesn't bother your husband?"

Pamela laughed and artfully dodged the question. "I know he *thinks* it'd be easier if we shared the exact same thoughts on every issue." But that wasn't about to happen, and they both knew it.

An hour later, Jessica and Mark walked to the car. He drove her to Gloria Rothschild's residence. Their second initial interview also went smoothly.

"How did you and the senator meet?" Jessica inquired.

Looking in perfect health and completely in control of the situation, Gloria answered with a gracious smile, "My father was supporting his campaign. Smitten with both his looks and his commanding personality, I volunteered to work on his campaign. The night he won the election was the night we became engaged, and we were married three months after he took office."

Some of this Jessica already knew, but she wanted to cover every base. It also helped to get the story in Gloria's own words. And it helped to bond her to them. "Your parents approved of the marriage?"

"Oh, yes. What was there not to approve of? Douglas was from a very wealthy family, too. He'd gone to Ivy League schools. My parents were delighted to have him as their son-in-law."

"The past three campaigns you haven't been very active." She had smiled and stood at her husband's side, but unlike other political wives, she hadn't gone off on her own to stump for her husband. Jessica couldn't help but wonder if this presented a problem for the senator.

Briefly Gloria looked troubled as she quietly admitted, "I have a fear of public speaking. My husband understands and accepts my shyness. He doesn't expect me to do more."

Mark reloaded his camera. "Ever think about seeing someone for that shyness?" he asked calmly.

Gloria palmed the pearls around her neck. "I did, a long while back. The hypnotherapy didn't help. Avoiding public speaking engagements did. So now I no longer have a problem."

They all smiled. But Jessica couldn't help thinking: *Maybe, maybe not.*

"SO WHAT DO WE HAVE?" Mark asked several hours later, as they reviewed their notes, along with the packet of previously published material on the two women the agency had gathered for them.

"As far as Gloria and Pamela go, they're both political liabilities to their husbands. Gloria because she refuses to campaign for her husband. Pamela because she takes public stands on controversial matters that her husband often avoids. Both are from monied backgrounds."

"And both have children that are almost grown." Mark switched on the evening news and came back to sit beside her on the sofa.

"Who do we have set up to interview tomorrow?"

"Only Senator Webb's wife so far."

"I guess that means we better get on it then," Mark said.

Jessica's attention was caught as without warning Craig Rothschild's picture flashed onto the screen. Mark went over swiftly to turn up the sound.

"—arrested today for the murder of known drug dealer, Vinnie Forsythe. He was found at the scene with a syringe in one hand, a gun in the other, apparently attempting to make it look like a drug-related suicide. The senator's son is being held without bail...."

Jessica looked at Mark, her pulse racing. She didn't know yet how exactly, but clearly Craig was involved in this, too. Maybe by talking to him they could find out more about Suzette's death. "Can we get in to see him?" As simple journalists, it would normally be impossible, but Mark had connections that were a dream come true—for a reporter, anyway.

Mark nodded, looking as much intrigued as perplexed. "I'll call Noah. He'll pull some strings."

"Hell, no, I didn't do it!" Craig sobbed as they met with him in the small windowless jail room in Arlington, Virginia. "Not that my dad will ever believe me."

"He's been to see you?" Jessica asked gently.

"Been here and left!" Now Craig sobbed openly, cradling his head on his folded arms. "He said I could rot here, for all he cared!"

"I thought you were supposed to be in seclusion until your trial on the drug charges," Mark interjected, coming on to Craig like an older brother. To Jessica the act didn't seem at all false. He behaved, at the moment anyway, like a truly compassionate person. But he could also be hard and tough, she reminded herself firmly, determined not to let herself take a too rose-tinted view of the CIA agent.

"I was." Craig sniffed. "But then I got this call, from a guy who said he knew something about Suzette's murder. He told me when and where to meet him. And when I got there, that Vinnie guy was already dead."

"And that's when the police showed up," Jessica surmised, this time letting the tape recorder in her purse take the notes for her.

Craig nodded. "Somebody called them, too."

"So you think you were set up?" Mark asked.

Craig looked at him angrily. "Of course I was set up!

"Did you tell the police this?" Jessica asked. "Your father?"

"They don't believe me. They think it's the drugs, that I was just trying to buy more and that something went wrong." He gulped hard. "My dad even accused me of supplying Suzette with the drugs that killed her! As if I would ever do something like that! And all just because I'm a college student and partied too hard and flunked out of school—"

Was that why the senator was working so hard—albeit through Bennett—to quell any further investigation into Suzette's murder? Jessica wondered. Because they both thought his son had killed her?

"Craig, where did Suzette get those drugs, assuming for a moment she bought them herself—and that they weren't just planted on her?" Jessica asked.

"I don't know. Vinnie probably. The guy was a walking drugstore. Why? Do you think she was murdered, too?"

"Maybe." Jessica paused, wondering how much Craig knew. There was also the chance he knew more than he was aware of. "How involved were you with Suzette?" Jessica asked.

Craig was quiet for a long moment as he wiped the tears from his face. "I was in love with her," he said finally in the dejected tone of an unacknowledged suitor.

"And how did she feel about you?"

Craig looked at Jessica resentfully. "You're her friend, you ought to know. She didn't even know I was alive—except," he amended wearily, "maybe in the terms of a kid brother. Yeah, I guess that about sums it up. She thought I was a kid."

And at nineteen, he considered himself a man, Jessica was sure.

"We want to help you," Mark interjected levelly.

Craig's gaze grew cynical. "And get a story out of it."

Mark didn't deny it. "Every dog's gotta have his day."

"Yeah." Craig was silent, not disputing that, either. He looked at them both abruptly, his earnestness evident and indisputable. "I swear to you both, I didn't kill him. I was there. I walked into a trap, but I didn't kill him."

The funny thing was, Jessica believed him.

Chapter Eleven

"You'll want to take a look at this," Mark said the following morning as she joined him for a room service breakfast.

He handed her the morning paper. On the front page was a picture of a handcuffed Audrey leaving Arlington police headquarters. "Senator Rothschild's Aide Provides Alibi for Son!" Jessica read the headline, stunned.

"Keep reading," Mark encouraged her, taking a seat at the breakfast table.

Audrey Moore, thirty-five, told police late yesterday that she was with Craig Rothschild when he received the call from Vinnie Forsythe at the senator's house. She followed Craig to the secluded area after noticing his distraught state, but she panicked and ran when she saw Vinnie was dead and that Craig had apparently walked into a trap. Another eyewitness, a jogger, told police he saw a dark-haired man of medium height and weight getting into a car with Vinnie Forsythe approximately twenty minutes before police arrived. The search for the killer is continuing, with police efforts now focused on finding the unidentified dark-haired man.

Anyone with information is asked to call police headquarters in Arlington.

Still stunned by the turn of events, Jessica looked over at Mark. "Craig didn't say anything about Audrey when we talked to him!"

"I know. That bothers me, too. As hysterical as he was last night about being in jail, I would've thought he'd have jumped at anything that would get him out."

Jessica munched on a piece of toast. "Maybe he never knew he was being followed."

Mark finished his eggs, clearly deep in thought.

"You don't think she'd lie about something like that?" Frowning, Jessica took a long sip of her coffee, grimacing as she discovered it was lukewarm.

Mark shrugged. "We both know how deep her loyalty to the senator runs, and she did get Craig out of jail."

"Any chance we can get in to see her?" Jessica asked, finishing the last of her toast and brushing the crumbs off her hands.

"We can try, but I doubt she'll talk to us."

Mark's hunch proved correct. Getting the bad news from another staffer at the senator's office, he said, "Okay, we'll assume she is lying for Craig. But if that eyewitness account of a dark-haired man seen with Vinnie holds up, she'll be redeemed by the press. She saved a life."

Jessica nodded. "Craig was lucky on this one. Two came forward in support, even if one is biased. I'm sure he's innocent of the charges, anyway—"

Before she could complete the thought, the phone jangled.

No sooner had Jessica picked it up than she realized it was her boss, in an aggrieved mood. "*The Spring Valley Sentinel* may not be the big time, Jessica, but it is a working newspaper. And working newspapers need working reporters. I agreed to the leave of absence because I thought you had some loose ends to tie up. I didn't agree to it so you could run off and free-lance on the East Coast with some hotshot photographer!"

Jessica felt as though her heart was breaking. She'd never wanted to hurt the people she worked with in Spring Valley. *Damn it,* that was her home! "Mac, you don't understand—"

"The hell I don't. I know a money-grubbing opportunist when I see one! Twenty-four hours, Jessica. You've got twenty-four hours to get yourself back to Ohio and to your job. Or you're fired. *Comprende*?" There was a thud as Mac disconnected them.

Slowly Jessica put down the phone, becoming aware that Mark was watching her steadily.

"Trouble?"

"And then some. My boss found out I'm working here. I've got twenty-four hours to go back or I'm fired."

He shrugged, apparently unconcerned, perhaps feeling she'd be better off being fired. "So?"

"So that's my job."

"You can get another one," he reassured her calmly.

Could she? Suddenly, Jessica wasn't sure. The house in Spring Valley and her network of lifelong friends there provided all the security she had. "I have a house there. A mortgage. I can't just quit on the spur of the moment. My savings account won't support such flightiness."

His face softened compassionately. "So what are you going to do?" he asked gently.

"I'll call Mac back and explain what I'm doing." She reached for the receiver.

Quicker than lightning he was beside her, his hand stopping her action. "Wrong. You can't say anything to anyone about what you're doing."

Jessica wrested her hand free. "I can't let him think—"

"You have to," he interrupted her coldly.

"Mark!" She rose and stepped several feet back.

He stood silent, looking at her with obvious concern. "You can't jeopardize what we've learned so far," he said in a soft voice.

Jessica forced herself to consider his point of view. She could see that it would be a risk—an unnecessary one. She might put herself in danger, and she couldn't jeopardize Mark or his cover. It was enough that he'd told her who he was and trusted her to keep that secret. "You're right, of course," she admitted finally. "I can't tell Mac the truth, at least not now. However I will—" she gulped hard at the look on his face "—turn in my resignation and clear out my desk. Mac was right. It wasn't right for me to lie to him and it isn't fair to expect him to keep my position open indefinitely. There are at least ten people in the immediate vicinity who would jump at the chance to have that job...." She paused, wanting him to understand.

"All right," he said softly, accepting her decision. "Just as long as you remember we're going to stay in this until the mystery of Suzette's death is resolved."

"IT REALLY THREW YOU into a panic, didn't it, when your boss called and threatened to fire you?" Mark mused later that night as they finished the last of the pizza they'd ordered.

Jessica nodded, glad they'd returned to their hotel for dinner after an afternoon of more interviews, rather than go out again. "As determined as I am to find out what happened to Suzette, I really don't want to lose my job. I just wish I could have talked to Mac again today." But he'd been out and hadn't returned her call. Knowing she wouldn't be able to talk to him until business hours the following day made her feel even worse.

She could tell Mark didn't have the same need for overall stability she had, and that disappointed her in ways she hadn't expected. "Does that surprise you?"

After a moment he shook his head. "No, I could tell the first night I saw you there, in your home, how much the place meant to you."

Jessica flushed, surprised he'd noticed. "It's my history. I grew up there."

"Did you plan on going back there after college?"

"No, but my mother had gotten sick by then. And it just . . . I knew it was what I had to do. I haven't regretted it since."

His eyes darkened. "Maybe it's time to move on, Jessica."

She glanced down and away from his mesmerizing gaze. The more she looked deeply into his eyes, the more she felt she could drown in them. In him. She swallowed hard around the tight knot of emotion in her throat and forced herself to respond to his challenge. "I keep telling myself that," she admitted softly. "But a part of me doesn't want to let go." Just as another part of her didn't want to let go of Suzette's death.

He was silent, then picked up on what she hadn't said. "You've never talked about your father."

Without warning, bitterness filled her throat. There was a reason for that. "That's because there's not much to say, I guess. He was a glamorous, good-times sort of guy, who walked out on my mother and me when I was five, because he couldn't stand the staidness of married life."

They hesitated, each watching the other. "You've never gotten over it, have you?"

She flinched and looked away. "It's not easy to take, being abandoned like that."

"I'm sorry," he said quietly, covering her hand with his own.

"So was I—for a long time." Feeling restless, Jessica disengaged her hand for a moment, got up and moved to the window. Although she wanted to be home again, there was still so much for her to do in Washington. She felt impossibly torn.

She turned back to Mark, and because he seemed to want to know, she summed up how she felt about her father's leaving. "It's taken me a long time to come to grips with what he did, but as an adult, I now know it was for the best, that although I still think he took the easy way out, leaving couldn't have been easy for him, either. I'm sure he still has his guilt, just as I'm sure in the final analysis he only did what he felt he had to do, what was right for him, at least. My father never would have been happy in a small town. If he'd stayed, he would've made us miserable, too." And that Jessica probably couldn't have borne.

Mark stood and moved slowly to her side. He was so close that she had to tilt her head to look up at him; she could feel the heat emanating from his body and smell the warm, musky scent of his skin. "Your mother was good to you?"

"Oh, yes." Jessica smiled at the memory, recounting affectionately, "My mother was everything to me—mother, father, best friend, counselor. She was my biggest supporter and my harshest critic, and I owe everything I am to her." Without warning, Jessica missed her mother unbearably and her eyes filled with tears. She turned away, embarrassed, not wanting Mark to see.

Suddenly she was in his arms. He was kissing her as if he knew how to make the hurt go away. And the miracle of it was, he did....

FIVE HUNDRED MILES AWAY, Pamela Fieldler woke up slowly, in strange surroundings but with a familiar feeling of terror. She was in a hotel room. She didn't know how she got there, or why, or even the name of the hotel.

The same thing had happened before. Several times.

She was frightened. She couldn't figure out what triggered these episodes, the loss of control; nor could she remember precisely when each blackout began. All she knew was that they were happening with increasing frequency.

As before, she was dressed to seduce in the kind of slinky outfit she'd never be caught dead in. Her nightgown was made of minimal amounts of ice-green satin and a great deal of peekaboo lace. A matching negligee, feather boa and feather-trimmed slippers lay scattered across the carpet, along with several silk scarves. Flavored body oils stood on the nightstand. The bed sheets were rumpled. There was an empty magnum of champagne lying nearby. She swore, lamenting her lack of judgment and what foolishness might have followed.

She had to get out of here before she was discovered. With a throbbing headache and dry mouth, she staggered to the bathroom to dress.

MARK TOSSED AND TURNED on the sofa. Try as he might, he was unable to sleep. Every time he shut his eyes he thought about the kiss, and the way he'd responded to her vulnerability.

It wasn't usual behavior for him. Generally, he could remain emotionally uninvolved, no matter how traumatic or trying the situation. That was what made him so good in the field. But his reaction to Jessica had been anything but unemotional. She'd touched him from the start. He'd wanted to comfort her at the funeral, but had contented himself with taking photographs. He'd talked to her only briefly at the wake and had left wanting more. After that he'd followed her around, hating the way his job had forced him to intrude on her grief.

He knew she felt whatever was happening between them, too. But then the problems would loom. And the problems, the Suzette Howar murder mystery aside, weren't likely to go away.

He sighed and shifted onto his side. It was unlike him to borrow trouble.

He needed to take things one day at a time, not think about the future. But with lovely Jessica sleeping right next door in a long white flannel nightgown, it was easier said than done.

"YOU'RE LEAVING the *Sentinel* for good, aren't you?" Mac asked early the next morning, before Jessica was even halfway through her apology.

Jessica cradled the telephone in her hand, wishing there were some other way. "I realized when we talked yesterday that I couldn't keep you hanging on indefinitely, and at this point I don't know when I'll be back." Her throat was tight with suppressed emotion as she finished.

"Does your absence have something to do with that guy you've been hanging around lately—who'd Bennett say he was—Mark Galahad?"

"Gallagher," she corrected reflexively.

"Or is it your friend's death that's put you in a tailspin?" Mac continued.

"Maybe a little bit of both," she said honestly, the regret she felt at leaving her job echoing in her tone.

Mac swore. "I'm going to hate to lose you."

"I know. I'll come back and visit." But she wouldn't be able to live there unless she had a job.

"Lady, you better," Mac commented gruffly, then ended the conversation on a peaceful, accepting note.

At least Mac was no longer angry with her, Jessica thought, relieved.

"Change frightens you, doesn't it?" Mark commented, coming back into the room just as she hung up.

Jessica nodded, knowing there was no way he couldn't have noticed the strain on her face. "I'm used to knowing exactly where I belong." She regarded his easygoing expression, her bafflement evident. "You feel the opposite, don't you?"

He nodded, his eyes never leaving hers. "I guess I'm what you'd call a rolling stone. I can't stand to let any grass grow under me." He removed his camera from the case and began to clean the exterior with a blower brush.

"Why?" Jessica watched him work, mesmerized by the graceful movements of his hands.

"I don't know." Mark shrugged. "Part of it is I'm restless by nature. The other half may have to do with my youth." At her curious look, he explained further, "I've got an IQ of 152 but I was what you might call a problem child," he said wryly, picking up a silicone cloth.

"How so?"

"How so? Bored all the time, I suppose." Gently he rubbed the exterior of the camera with the soft cloth, carefully removing every smudge. "Having to sit in a class day after day while my teacher explained addition to the other children was unbearable, so I found other ways to amuse myself."

"Such as?"

He grinned again, laughing softly. "Putting frogs in the girls' toilet. Writing every letter in the alphabet backward on my papers. Making up my own language and sharing it with the other kids. For a while the teacher thought we were all mentally deficient."

Jessica grinned, amused. "You must've been a terror."

"I was. Until the sixth grade, anyway. Then they got me in appropriate classes, gave me incredible amounts of intellectually challenging work to do, and generally kept me busy most of the time."

"But you were still unhappy," she guessed.

He nodded. "I sensed something was missing. My parents were both architects and encouraged me to put more emphasis on the social aspect of school. So I became active in student government. I played football and basketball and excelled at both. Next I joined the debate team and played drums in the school band."

"But you were still not challenged enough."

"Which was when I took up photography." He added a few drops of cleaner to a special lens-cleaning tissue and gently wiped the lens.

"You must've been something."

"I was that all right." Mark opened the film chamber and carefully dusted out the inside.

She realized it was the first time he'd ever told her much of anything about himself—maybe because at the moment he was so preoccupied with his camera. "So how did you end up in your current job?" she asked.

"I was recruited in college. I had planned to go to law school, but then this opportunity came along. Thinking about it, I realized I'd drive myself crazy if I had to sit cooped up in an office all day, and although the courtroom theatrics might appeal to me if I worked in criminal law, there were too many other drawbacks to make it worthwhile for me. So I took the job that would challenge me in every way. And it has done just that."

"How did your parents feel about it?"

He grinned again and placed a new roll of film in the camera. "They like the fact I'm a photographer for *Personalities*."

Even his family didn't know what he did. Jessica was simultaneously touched and amazed that he had trusted her with his real identity. "What would they think if they knew?"

"My mother would worry herself to death," he said flatly. "So would my dad. So I'm content with things as is."

The question was, Jessica mused, would she ever be? If she became involved with Mark, could she live with seeing him only when time and opportunity and his work allowed?

She didn't know. And until she did, maybe it was better not to get more deeply involved with him than she already was.

Chapter Twelve

"Face it," Jessica said as they breakfasted together in their DC hotel suite. "We've tried our best, but we're at a dead end." They'd spent the last two days interviewing and photographing other subjects, to no avail. None of the other political wives seemed to know Suzette at all, though they had been mentioned in her journal. Whatever Suzette thought she had uncovered was still not clear to them. And although Jessica had wracked her brain trying to figure out where Suzette might have hidden the rest of her manuscript—surely there were more than one hundred pages after nearly four years of effort!—she had yet to come up with anything concrete. *So much for Suzette's suggestion to look into their shared past,* she reflected wryly.

"No, we're not, although it may very well seem to you like we're at a dead end. But you're right. As far as the investigation goes, we are in trouble," Mark countered reasonably, pouring them both some more coffee. "We need to go back to square one and review what we already know, start off at the beginning again on a different path."

What he said made sense, and she began to relax.

"What was she like personally? Extravagant? Independent?"

"Well, she was frugal when it came to mundane tasks. Going to a grocery store with her was like shopping with a miser. But she was extravagant in areas like clothes, car, furniture. She wanted it to look as if she lived very well. The trappings of success were important to her."

"What were her favorite subjects in school?"

"English and history. She was lousy at math. It made her furious that she couldn't even do her tax returns." Suddenly, the inspiration they had been looking for hit. "That's it!" Snapping her fingers, Jessica sat up quickly.

"What?"

"She didn't do her own tax returns!"

Mark furrowed his brow. "You think she tried to deduct her writing expenses?"

"Not yet. There's a law saying you can't do that until you make a profit; she hadn't sold anything yet. But she was probably keeping track of her expenses."

"To deduct retroactively once the project sold."

"Right. And her accountant would have that information."

"I'm betting on it." Jessica smiled triumphantly.

"Do you know who her accountant was?" Jessica shook her head. "Well, it doesn't matter. We can find out," Mark continued, heading for the phone. Using his CIA connections, he got the information. Minutes later they were on their way.

Harold Shelton was a quiet unassuming man with a receding hairline and a potbelly. He had a small suburban office in Gaithersburg, Maryland. In his late forties, he was about as far removed from the fast lane as it was possible to get.

"Oh yeah, she was keeping records, all right. Her expenses were pretty heavy, too."

"What was she spending money on?" Jessica wanted to know.

Harold Shelton consulted his records. "Research trips to New York. She did a lot of photocopying in the New York City library on weekends. And she was buying a lot of hardcover research books, too."

"About what?"

"You can see the list of titles for yourself." Mr. Shelton pulled the appropriate page from the file and slid it toward her.

Jessica frowned. "These are all about drugs."

"We keep coming back to her fascination with chemical substances, don't we?" Mark asked, perplexed.

"I read about her death in the paper. A shame. She didn't seem like someone who was on drugs," Mr. Shelton said.

"She wasn't," Jessica said briskly. But it seemed more and more evident they were investigating someone who did have a drug problem. That was the only explanation that made any sense. At any rate, Jessica knew she would never be able to rest, nor would Mark, until they filled in all the missing pieces of this puzzle. *Damn it,* they had to find the rest of her manuscript. The question was; where had Suzette hidden it?

"WHEN IT RAINS it pours. Now I've got two reasons to go to New York," Mark said, hanging up the phone just as Jessica finished packing her suitcase. By mutual agreement they were taking the shuttle to New York, where they would stay for the next day or so.

"That was the magazine?"

"Right. *Personalities* is doing an article on Audrey. She's going to be next week's cover story. They want the photos taken at Suzette's funeral. The negatives are in my apartment. I'll have to develop them and get them to the office by tomorrow morning at nine o'clock."

"Are you going to interview her?"

"My boss only wishes that were possible. No. Audrey's gone into seclusion for a few days. Apparently the senator wants her out of the reach of reporters until this whole business blows over."

Jessica glanced at her watch. *Barely noon.* They had time to catch the shuttle and still be in New York as they'd originally planned by late afternoon. "How long will it take you to do the pictures?"

"Not long. Maybe an hour. We'll do our other researching first."

Their tenacity paid off. Not only were they able to confirm Suzette's presence at the New York library, but had an opportunity to talk to the head reference librarian, who remembered Suzette well. "Oh sure. I remember Ms. Howar," she began, after taking them back to a small private conference room. "She was really into all that Capitol glitz."

"What do you mean?" Jessica asked.

"That's what she was researching. Prominent families in Washington, socialites, women with tragic pasts in particular. What was she working on, anyway? Something for Senator Rothschild?"

Not exactly. "We're not sure," Jessica responded as honestly as possible. "That's what we're trying to figure out. Do you remember her looking up anything else?"

"Well, for a while she was on a real self-improvement kick. Read everything she could find about dieting, how to increase one's self-esteem and take charge of your own life. How to find personal happiness, books like that.''

Suzette? Into self-help literature? Somehow that just didn't fit. As long as Jessica had known her, she'd always felt Suzette was perfectly happy the way she was. In fact, she'd always eschewed that type of book!

''Did she ever say anything to indicate what had prompted her to read all those books, or if studying them helped her in any way?'' Jessica asked.

The librarian shook her head.

''Did she ever mention plans to write a biography of Senator Rothschild?'' Mark asked.

''No, not a word, and I'd have remembered that!''

Jessica was sure she would, too.

As they left the library, Mark and Jessica ruminated on what they knew about Suzette's dealings in New York. ''I still think Tamara North was lying to me when she said Suzette was planning to write a biography of Senator Rothschild for his presidential bid.''

''There's only one way to find out,'' Mark said determinedly.

When they called to get an appointment with Tamara though, they found out she was out of town for the next two weeks, doing business on the West Coast. That, however, didn't deter Mark. From a coffee shop across the street, they watched for her secretary, waiting until she'd left the office for the day.

Soon after, Mark and Jessica were inside the office building. Since it was nearing five o'clock, they had no trouble using the elevator to Tamara's floor. ''We're going to be caught breaking and entering, I know it,'' Jessica moaned as Mark worked on freeing the simple lock.

"We're lucky she doesn't have a burglar alarm system."

Sweaty moments later, they were finally in. Mark shut the door quietly behind them, then carefully resecured the lock. "Better not turn on any lights," he whispered, walking as stealthily on the polished wooden floors as if he were barefoot.

Outside darkness was already falling, but they had just enough light to see by. "Remember, we want absolutely no sign that anyone was here. Put everything back exactly as you found it."

"I will," Jessica promised.

While Mark started on the file cabinets, Jessica looked at the appointment calendar on Tamara's desk. Nowhere did she find any evidence that Suzette had scheduled an appointment with Tamara, but two days before Suzette died, the literary agent had met with one Bennett Agee for half an hour.

Jessica was in shock. Had Bennett found out what her friend was up to and killed Suzette? But how was that possible? He'd been in Ohio at the time of her death. Jessica had taken the last plane out that night, and he hadn't been on it.

Nonetheless, she had to face the possibility that if Bennett Agee had known about Tamara North and Suzette's tell-all book, he might have had a part in Suzette's death.

She showed Mark what she'd found. He, too, stared grimly at the entry. "I knew that guy wasn't telling us everything he knew," Mark muttered. Then, taking Jessica's hand, he led her toward the opposite end of the office. "I've got something to show you, too."

Filed under Suzette was a file of correspondence on Suzette Howar. "She must be keeping this to cover herself, in case there is any trouble," Mark whispered, handing Jessica half the file for perusal. It included Suzette's contract with Tamara and related material. "It says here that Tamara accepted Suzette as a client over two years ago!" Jessica whispered.

"Here's a letter from Suzette dated last fall," Mark murmured. "She says she still has no idea where the manuscript is going or how it will end."

"And here's a carbon copy reply from Tamara, urging her to continue."

"What's the date on that?"

"November."

"Anything more recent?"

"Wait a minute. Here's one that was sent out December 15. Tamara is urging her to continue on the book, says that she's still very excited about it and is going to read the rough draft of the book's middle section over Christmas vacation."

"The only question now is; where are those pages?"

Jessica glanced at the rows of boxed manuscripts on the floor-to-ceiling shelves lining one whole wall of the office. It was going to be a long night.

For the next hour and a half they checked every white cardboard box on the shelves—to no avail. Suzette's book was nowhere to be found. "Maybe she destroyed the pages," Jessica theorized glumly.

"I don't think so." Mark went back to take a second look at the files where he'd found the correspondence. "She had to know she was sitting on a potential gold mine, especially after the sensational way Suzette died. Forget for a second whether the work is salable in a literary or commercial sense or even halfway readable—it would sell a certain amount of copies, just because people would want to know what Suzette had been writing."

"And as her agent, Tamara would probably get ten to fifteen percent of the profits?"

"You've got it."

That meant the manuscript was probably somewhere in the office. A tense hour later, they found it filed under *D*—"Dreams of Glory." "Let's get out of here," Mark said, already covering their tracks and making sure everything was exactly as they'd found it. "We'll take the book back to my place." He slipped it inside his bomber jacket and zipped up the front.

Jessica nodded, excitement roaring through her veins. She couldn't wait to read what they'd found.

"SHE'S MAKING A FOOL out of herself," Senator Rothschild said, as he watched Pamela Fieldler hold court on the other side of the Fieldler living room.

"So what's new?" Bennett asked sarcastically, sipping his tonic water and wishing for a double of prime Kentucky whiskey.

"Though what she's trying to prove—" Senator Rothschild broke off and angrily turned away.

Bennett looked back at Pamela Fieldler. She was in rare form that evening, vocally supporting the theory that a man's house was his castle, and his wife there only to serve him. "It's the champagne talking," he said, forcing himself to be pleasant.

"Everyone here knows how she really feels about everything from the Equal Rights Amendment to abortion."

"And that's precisely why she's spouting off with the opposite," Bennett said, returning his boss's thin-lipped smile. "Can't you see the laughs she's getting?"

"With my wife Gloria the most amused," the senator continued bleakly.

"At least *she's* not drinking," Bennett said. In the past, the problem had been trying to keep Gloria reasonably sober—at least until they got her home. Because once she started, she wasn't easy to stop.

"I suppose I can be thankful for that much." The senator sighed and was quiet. "Did she tell you where she was earlier? I saw you talking to her when she came in."

"She said she saw Craig."

Senator Rothschild's face assumed a worried look. "And?"

"And she's worried about him, too," Bennett reported sympathetically, taking another sip of tonic. "She said she'll do anything she can to see he's kept out of jail. The problem is, she just doesn't know what to do."

"There's nothing to do. The charges against him were dropped." Senator Rothschild took comfort in that.

"The way he's been behaving, she's afraid he'll get into trouble again."

Across the room, Pamela Fieldler poured herself two more glasses of champagne. She sipped it voluptuously, drinking first from one glass, then the other. "Women should be put on a pedestal," she continued, leaning against the baby grand. "My husband's certainly put me on one."

"That's it," Senator Fieldler said, speaking to no one in particular, his face creased and angry. "I'm getting her out of here, even if I have to carry her kicking and screaming."

Senator Rothschild and Bennett were of one mind on that. They both stepped forward to stop their friend and colleague. "Don't," Senator Rothschild counseled. "You'll just make it worse. Let her blow off some steam. She'll wind down eventually. We've all been under a tremendous strain lately."

Even before he finished speaking, Senator Rothschild watched with satisfaction and relief as his own wife started forward to rescue Pamela. But Pamela Fieldler refused to surrender her glass. Sparked to anger, she jerked her arm away, sloshing vintage champagne all over the glossy surface of the piano. "No!" she said defiantly, her voice way too loud. "I will not stop!" She turned to glare rebelliously at her husband. "It relaxes me." She smiled, her tone growing strange and mysterious, almost sultry. "And my husband likes me relaxed." Slowly, ever so slowly, she put her glass aside. Swaying seductively, she started toward the embarrassed senator from Indiana. "He doesn't want me to dance, but he likes me physically fit. Don't you, honey?"

"Pamela—" Her husband ground out her name through tightly clenched teeth.

Ignoring the warning, Pamela walked past her husband and pushed open the double French doors to the atrium. Her stride never slowing, she stepped purposefully to the water's edge and dived in.

She surfaced moments later looking like a wet rat, having lost some of her jewelry and her shoes. She smiled at her husband and cocked her head at a mischievous angle. "Satisfied, darling?"

Bennett stared at her, knowing he'd never seen anything as outrageous. Senator Fieldler's aides would have to work double time to keep his wife's antics out of the paper. Of course, the senator was furious. But Pamela seemed not to care as she stripped off her evening dress and began to swim laps. *What is wrong with her?* Bennett wondered. He'd never seen her act so bizarre, out of character even for her. What would Senator Fieldler do if his wife really was as crazy as she appeared?

His boss was right. Gloria needed to stay as far away from Pamela as possible. With the senator planning to run for the presidency, any hint of madness could be deadly. Not just for his career, but for them all.

Chapter Thirteen

Her hands trembling as she finished the last sections, Jessica stared at the manuscript. There were the next hundred pages of "Dreams of Glory," as well as the first portion that she and Mark had already read. It appeared that for safety's sake, Suzette had divided her manuscript into three parts. But where was the third and final portion that would tie up all the loose ends?

Setting the thought aside, Jessica began to read. In tone the first two parts were very different. Instead of depicting the heroine witnessing bizarre behavior among some wives of the social "in" set, this portion portrayed a bittersweet love story. And—a stunning revelation—it was clear the characters were Suzette and Senator Rothschild.

Suzette and the senator lovers? Jessica marveled. She could hardly believe it. He seemed to be such a family man! Not the kind who'd take advantage of a young innocent on his staff. The heroine—and she suspected Suzette, too—had dropped the distinguished-looking older "gentleman" when she learned he was a philanderer.

Jessica knew this happened in Washington. It happened everywhere there were successful older men and vulnerable ambitious young women. Power was a great aphrodisiac. Still...

"I feel so sorry for her," Jessica whispered, still stunned as she looked at Mark. How was it, as close as the two women had been, that Jessica had never suspected, never guessed? Had Suzette been too embarrassed to admit it...? "I mean, how humiliating to think you've found true love, albeit illicit, and then discover you're just one more in a series of conquests." Jessica pushed the manuscript pages away from her, suddenly finding them distasteful.

Mark sympathized, his look equally troubled. "From what she wrote, it sounds like he knew just what to say to a young girl."

"The louse. He probably used the same lines on all of them. Lines that were suavely perfect at his age!" Jessica wiped away her angry tears, consoling herself with another thought. "At least Suzette finally got wise. At least she dumped him!"

"Yeah. *That* must've been a jolt to his ego."

Jessica was silent, realizing the implication of what Mark had said. "Mark—" Her voice was shaking as the next thought came. "You don't think...the senator...is it possible he was involved in Suzette's death?"

Mark was silent. "It's always a possibility...but with him planning to run for president, I just don't think he'd take the risk. Besides, according to the book, the affair happened during Suzette's early days in Washington. Quite a lot of time has elapsed since then. More likely than not, what happened between them was a closed issue by the time she died."

Jessica sighed. Mark was right. It didn't make sense for the senator to risk killing Suzette now, when he was preparing to launch a national campaign, especially not over an affair that was long over. He wouldn't want to do anything to draw negative attention to himself, nor to anyone on his staff.

"What about his wife? Gloria?"

Again Mark looked hesitant. "I don't know. Maybe. I guess it's possible she found out about the affair and hired someone to knock Suzette off, making it look like a suicide. It was a professional hit. But again, that's an awful lot of trouble to go to for an affair that was long over, and Suzette wasn't the only woman in her husband's life. It seems to me if she wanted to kill someone, it'd be his current mistress, whoever it was, not an old flame who'd dumped him."

"And it couldn't have been Craig. He was in love with her himself."

"I agree. I could be wrong, but from where I stand . . . Craig just doesn't have what it takes to murder someone, or even hire to have it done."

Which left them with no suspects. Again.

Jessica felt the color draining from her face. She wished Suzette had never come to Washington. She wished she were here now, so they could talk about all that had happened. But that wasn't possible. There was only one thing Jessica could do.

I'll find your murderer, she promised her friend grimly. *I'll find him or her and see them punished, if it is the last thing I ever do. . . .*

THE NEXT HALF HOUR passed morosely in silence as both Jessica and Mark reviewed all they had discovered. Finally he couldn't take it anymore—the helplessness, the anger, the horrible sensation of watching Jessica feel so hurt, when there wasn't anything he could do or say that would really comfort her. It would simply take time for her wounds to heal, and time was what they had so little of now....

He jumped up from the sofa, aware he needed to do something. Anything. His apartment on Sixty-Second Street had never felt so claustrophobic to him before. He wondered how she must see his place, curled up unhappily as she was, in one corner of the sofa.

Small and sparsely furnished, the three rooms suited his needs—a bedroom for sleeping, a darkroom for developing his photos, a combination kitchen and living area for everything else. But seeing it through Jessica's eyes, he realized just how empty it was. Except for a few of his photos, which were framed and hanging on the wall, the prewar apartment was devoid of personality. It was a place to crash between assignments, nothing more, and contrasted harshly with her own home in Ohio.

For the first time in days, he felt the difference between them—and their life-styles—acutely. And he knew by the faintly disillusioned look on her face as, coming out of her funk, she finally glanced around, that she felt it, too.

"Hungry?" he asked, stalking into the kitchen. He rummaged through the refrigerator for something edible. Disgusted, he threw out a week-old carton of Hunan fish and hot sauce. He opened the cabinet. Nothing but a can of sliced mushrooms and a tin of mandarin oranges.

Jessica glided forward to stand next to him. A bemused smile on her face, she glanced into his refrigerator, her eyes lingering on the carton of eggs sitting next to several cans of beer, then let out a lengthy sigh that let him know just how bone-tired she was. "Are the eggs fresh?"

"Bought last week."

The smile widened slightly, giving her mouth an appealing shape. She tilted her head at him. "I make a mean omelet."

"With mushrooms and cheese?"

Jessica nodded. "You find the skillet. I'll break the eggs."

They worked in companionable silence. Mark opened beers for both of them. Their shoulders touched more than once, as they moved from stove to counter in the cramped space. Seeing her shiver faintly at the contact, it was all Mark could do not to take her into his arms and kiss her. Fortunately for both of them, the thought of how lovemaking might complicate their situation was enough to put on the brakes—at least for now.

They took their plates to the table. Their knees touched, and he scooted back. He could see Jessica searching for a topic of less depressing conversation—anything but Suzette. "You've lived here long?" she asked finally in a pleasant tone.

For some reason Mark liked the idea of making small talk with her in the intimacy of his place. He liked having her there. "About seven years, since I started working for the magazine." And except for the darkroom, which was expertly outfitted and complex, the place still looked as if he had moved in yesterday.

She looked around as if she liked it, anyway. "You like New York?"

He liked her. "I like the city."

"Why?" Her eyes looked very clear and blue in the soft light of his apartment, her hair shone like soft spun gold, and it was all he could do to suppress a stirring of desire.

"Because of the pace, the excitement, the changes." Mark forced his voice into a noncommittal tone.

She smiled again, and regaining her appetite, forked up the omelet they'd made together. "You found small-town life stifling?" Her tone was curious, intense.

"Don't you?" he asked casually. After all she was bright, energetic. Spring Valley was a fine place to raise a growing family or retire—not a place for a young woman several years out of school.

"Sometimes, but the cost of living isn't very high there. I own the family home—it became mine when my mother died—so I just have mortgage payments every month, taxes, insurance and utilities, which are very low."

So practical. This once he wanted her to be more impulsive. Impulsive enough to end up in his arms. He captured her hand with his, infusing it with strength. "Don't you ever want to do anything more challenging? Work at a bigger paper, for instance?"

She nodded, smiling, glad he'd picked up on that. "I've been trying to free-lance for magazines, but as yet I haven't had a whole lot of luck. A few articles published regionally, nothing on the national level."

"Yet," he repeated, knowing she had the drive, intelligence and tenacity to make it if she wanted to.

She ducked her head, blushing slightly. He could see his praise had touched her. And that left him feeling guilty. Because he knew when it came right down to it that he shouldn't let them get any closer. He didn't want her depending on him for anything more than the here and now, for survival. He didn't want to let her down, not now, not ever. And if he let her start depending on him emotionally, then he would hurt her. Just as surely as the senator in Suzette's novel had hurt Daisy.

Finished, he abruptly pushed back his chair and carried his dishes to the sink. Alert to the unhappy change in his mood, his new tenseness, she finished her meal in wary silence.

"I'm going into the darkroom." Once more his tone was gruff.

She was on her feet immediately. "Wait up and I'll help you."

"It isn't necessary—"

"I think it is," she insisted. "I want to see the pictures of Audrey you told me you took."

What could he say to that? Again he found himself wanting to kiss her, to pull her into his arms and never let go. There was a brief silence between them. "Come on, then," he said, irritated that he was having more trouble controlling his desires than a teenager.

If he'd found the apartment confining in her presence, he found the eight-by-ten area of his darkroom almost unbearable. Her essence was everywhere—a faint fragrance of flowers mixed with the soap-and-water scent of her skin and the shampoo-fresh smell of her hair. She was quiet, unobtrusive, yet always there to lend a hand whenever he needed it, seeming to know by instinct when to help, and when to simply get out of the way and watch. By the time they'd finished, it was 3:00 a.m. The photos of Audrey were drying on a clothesline strung across the room. There were three he felt were suitable for the magazine. In them, Audrey was watching the funeral stoically, without emotion, without a sign of grief. But then so was almost everyone else he had photographed.

"Only Craig and I were grieving deeply that day, weren't we?" Jessica asked softly.

"Suzette didn't have many friends."

She turned away, looking white and drained. Suddenly he couldn't help himself. He was reaching for her, drawing her into his arms. He meant just to hold her, to make her feel better, if only for a second. But then her head tilted back, she looked up into his eyes, and he lowered his mouth over hers.

The first touch of his lips to hers was electric, sparking a fire in him he felt in every inch of his body. She murmured her complaisance and melted against him, into him. His arms tightened around her, and he pulled her close, until her softness was a warm seductive blanket draped across the tensile length of his frame.

The kiss deepened and with a groan he forced her away from him. Her breathing as ragged as his, she stared up at him. She didn't have to ask why he'd stopped. She knew.

SHE'D MADE A FOOL of herself, Jessica thought as she curled up on his bed between plain white sheets under a dark blue blanket. After the kiss, he had decided it would be faster and more efficient for him to finish cleaning up the darkroom. She could hardly blame him for that. She knew better than to throw herself at a man, and yet she had done just that in his darkroom, kissing him as if there were no tomorrow. She knew part of it was the situation, the strain she had been under, her need to forget and to drift in a pleasant limbo of desire—and fulfillment. But that wasn't reason enough to complicate their relationship. What she was feeling for Mark went deeper than the physical, went further than the temporary partnership they had forged.

She was simply fascinated by the man. It was partly a result of his kindness to her. But it was also mixed up with the mystery of him and the taste of the forbidden—the fact was he was smart and clever, bold and courageous, sure of himself and seemingly of her. She could easily fall in love with him.

And he could easily fall in love with her. She saw it in his eyes. But she also knew Mark was far too pragmatic a person to let something that unwise happen. It was a sensitive and smart move on his part. And one part of her, a large part, was grateful for it. Another part of her, though, a small but insistent part, resented his ability to step back for a moment, to just walk away, when all she had wanted was to give in.

Frustrated beyond measure, she rolled over onto her stomach and plumped up the pillow with her fist. Unexpectedly she inhaled the scent of his after-shave. She groaned as unbidden memories of him came to mind.

It was going to be a long night. A very long night.

JESSICA AWAKENED to the aroma of freshly brewed coffee and the sounds of Mark showering in the tiny bathroom off the master bedroom. Startled to find she had fallen asleep, after all, despite her determination not to do so until he returned, she was just getting up when he emerged from the bathroom clad only in his trousers, his hair sleeked back wetly from his forehead. "You're up. Good. I made a phone call to Washington. Bennett Agee has agreed to see us at noon, at his apartment. We can just about make it if we catch the ten o'clock shuttle."

Jessica knew without his explaining what he was up to. "You want to question him about Tamara North, don't you?—that appointment he had with her two days before Suzette died."

"Don't you?"

She did and she didn't. "Bennett and I go way back," she said honestly, hedging. "I've known him years longer than I ever knew Suzette."

Mark stopped throwing clothes into a suitcase. "Which means what? That he's not a killer?"

"Just because he went to see Tamara North—"

"I don't think—" she swallowed hard "—he couldn't. He's not capable of that."

Mark moved closer, his stockinged feet soundless on the carpeted floor. "Everyone is capable of murder," he said quietly, his eyes never leaving hers, "if they are pushed or threatened enough. Just by writing her book, Suzette threatened the senator. If the senator's job was in jeopardy, then so was Bennett's. And we know if he visited Tamara North, then he knew Suzette was working on a tell-all exposé."

"I still don't believe it," she insisted stubbornly. "Bennett may be devoted to the senator, but he is not a killer."

Mark's mouth thinned into a white line. "We'll see." He finished packing in silence.

Jessica showered quickly and used Mark's dryer to dry her hair. The messenger had come and gone by the time she emerged, fully dressed, from the bath, and he was impatient to be on their way to the airport.

They didn't speak as they got onto the plane. Finally, halfway to Washington, after drinks and bags of peanuts had been served, Jessica could stand it no longer. "You think I'm naive," she accused him in a low, disillusioned tone that mirrored the way she felt about almost everything these days.

Unexpectedly Mark reached over and held her hand. "I think you want to believe in the wrong people."

He tightened his grip, but despite the fact they were arguing, she had no wish for him to relinquish his hold on her; on the contrary, it felt good, and right somehow. Reassuring. She closed her eyes against the sudden burn of tears. "I just want it to be over," she whispered hoarsely, feeling the exhaustion of the last week and a half sweep over her.

"I know," Mark said, tightening his grip on her hand even more. "I know."

"I DON'T KNOW what this is all about. I'm not sure I want to know," Bennett began the moment Jessica and Mark stepped into his Georgetown apartment. With its black and white color scheme, the art deco look, the thoughtfully decorated suite was more of a home than his permanent residence in Ohio.

"Try Tamara North," Mark said in the same aggressive tone.

Bennett whitened. He looked at Jessica, as if to say she had betrayed him in the worst possible way by joining forces with Mark. "Who?"

"Tamara North, Suzette's literary agent," Jessica replied, angered to find Bennett was lying to her, pretending not to even recognize the name. "The one she secretly hired."

"We know you went to see her two days before Suzette was murdered."

"Suzette wasn't murdered. She committed suicide. As for how you think you know the rest—"

"Are you denying it's true?" Because of all they'd meant to one another in the past, Jessica wanted him to level with her, to make her faith in him justified.

"I'm admitting nothing," Bennett said quietly.

"Fine," Mark said, taking Jessica's arm. "Then we'll go to the police with what we know."

"Hold it," Bennett said before either of them could take two steps. "All right. I went to see her."

"About Suzette?" Jessica asked, her throat feeling very dry. Her hands were beginning to shake.

Bennett nodded slowly, his eyes meeting Jessica's in a look that was both honest and faintly pleading. Ignoring Mark altogether, he went on, "I found out through a friend of a friend that Suzette had been known to go to New York to lunch with Ms. North." He clenched his hands into fists at his sides. "I never trusted Suzette, her reasons for working in the senator's office. I wasn't about to let her ruin his career, and especially not for her own gain."

"Then the senator had something to hide?" Jessica asked. Feeling she had to sit down or risk falling, she sank onto the sofa.

"No, of course not." Bennett sat down beside her. "But you know as well as I how powerful the printed word is. Right or wrong, many people believe everything they read. And Suzette knew enough about the workings of the office to give anything she might say a certain authenticity. Add to that, she ran with a very fast crowd. I didn't want any of her salacious 'memoirs' rubbing off on the senator. So I went to see Ms. North and told her publication of any book that in any way linked Suzette to Senator Rothschild or his office would be followed by a multimillion-dollar libel suit—not just against the author, but all parties involved—the publisher, agent, everyone. Ms. North wisely decided to force Suzette to write an authorized biography in anticipation of his bid for the presidency—the kind of flattering portrait the senator and his family could wholeheartedly endorse. If Suzette refused, Tamara planned to drop Suzette as a client. I left her office sure everything was settled. In fact, I assumed that she had contacted Suzette and told her the deal was off, and that

that was why Suzette called you so frantically, why she took those drugs.''

"She didn't do drugs!"

"Jessica, you have to start facing facts. I know how close you were to her, but Suzette was no fairy-tale princess. She was a troubled young woman with an appalling lack of judgment! She visited Vinnie Forsythe—"

"Don't you find it strange Vinnie was murdered, too?"

"Deservedly so, from the way it looks. I read the police files on him, Jessica. He was a career criminal—with any number of enemies."

"Do you number yourself among them?" Mark baited him calmly with a crocodile smile.

Once again, Bennett clenched his hands into fists. Jessica knew it was taking all his self-control not to punch Mark in the mouth. "I'm not a murderer," Bennett said fiercely. "And unlike you, I don't take advantage of innocent women!"

"Bennett, I can take care of myself," Jessica cut in tiredly, realizing they had learned as much as they were going to. She got to her feet.

"Can you?" Bennett said icily, again looking back at Mark with a critical eye. "Sometimes I wonder."

THE TEMPERATURE had climbed above the freezing mark, and it was raining steadily when they left Bennett's apartment—turning what was left of the snow to a thick gray slush that coated the sidewalks and grass, and perfectly mirrored Jessica's mood. Mark dropped her off at the front door of the hotel. "I'll meet you up at the room after I park the car in the garage across the street."

Jessica was glad of the time alone. Since he had kissed her, there'd been a new tension between them. And as much as she tried, she knew she couldn't will the turmoil away.

Her mind still on the kiss and her passionate reaction to it, Jessica opened the door. A gasp caught in her throat as she took in the papers scattered everywhere.

She felt something move behind her, then the lights went out. Acting on pure instinct, Jessica stepped quickly aside. With her peripheral vision she saw the heavy suitcase coming toward her a second before it slammed into her shoulder blade and the side of her neck. Jessica felt an explosion of pain. All went black as the carpet rose up to meet her.

Chapter Fourteen

Audrey's hands were remarkably steady as she walked out the service entrance of the hotel and around the corner to a parking garage down the street. It was amazing, she thought, how much more confident she had become in the past few days. How much more capable. Before she'd been afraid of so many things. Now it seemed she could do anything that needed to be done. She'd gotten the room number where Mark was staying from Bennett Agee, and then waited outside until she figured the two would be out nosing around. Fortunately for her, that was the same time the maids cleaned the rooms. All she'd had to do was walk in as if she were staying there and dismiss the maids. In dark glasses, a low-brimmed rain hat and leather coat padded to give her a misleading amount of girth, she doubted they would recognize her, or even be able to give police a halfway decent description of her.

The room to herself, she'd had twenty minutes to go over everything. What she'd found hadn't pleased her. It was obvious that Jessica and Mark were planning to write the same kind of sleazy exposé Suzette Howar had been penning at the time of her death. *Fools.* Didn't they realize by now that was what had gotten Suzette killed?

Not that she wanted to kill Jessica or Mark. She didn't like blood. She didn't even know how to fire or wield a weapon.

But those were minor details, she thought as she climbed into the rented green sedan and turned the key. The ignition sprang to life.

Audrey glanced at her watch. *Two-thirty.* She had plenty of time to avoid the rush-hour traffic and get back home, where she was supposed to be. But before she did that, she would have to make a report to the man who was now pulling all the strings—the man with the solutions—the man who made her strong and protected her. The only man she'd ever been able to rely on.

Nervously she bit her lip. She hoped he wouldn't be angry with her for botching the break-in. He had wanted her to leave the mess, to let them know they were in danger. He hadn't wanted her to be seen. But she might have been, and by that nosy Jessica. She wondered vaguely if that meant Jessica would have to die, too. And if she herself would have to be the one to take care of it, messy or not.

She supposed she would find out soon enough. As soon as she met the man.

Her gloved hands tightened on the steering wheel. Although she wasn't looking forward to it, she knew she had to do whatever the man assigned her to do. Even if it meant cold-blooded murder.

"Jessica, my God, what happened? Are you all right?" Mark rushed into the hotel room.

Jessica struggled to sit up. She moaned as pain ricocheted through her arm and up into her neck. "Someone was here when I got back."

Mark helped her up and onto the sofa in the living room of the suite. He glanced around at the chaos left in the mugger's wake. "Did you get a good look at who it was?"

"No, but I think it may have been a woman. I caught the faint scent of hair spray or makeup—something that was cosmetic and feminine."

"What'd she hit you with?"

"A suitcase, I think—that big hard-sided one. I'm not sure."

"Here, let me get you some ice." He disappeared briefly down the hall. Coming back, he wrapped the ice in a towel, then pressed it to the side of her neck. "Better?" he asked after several minutes had passed.

She nodded, still feeling shaken up. "Shouldn't we call the police?"

"I'd rather inventory first, try and figure out what's missing."

An hour later, they'd restored order to the room. Not surprisingly, their photocopies of the journal and manuscript were missing, as well as the sketchy notes they'd made thus far on the Washington scene. "Thank goodness we had the foresight to put the originals into an agency vault for safekeeping," Jessica murmured. "But why would anyone want the master list of the political wives we intend to interview?" Jessica asked.

"Probably because we're on the right track, thinking that's why Suzette was killed—because she knew something about someone that the thief wouldn't want revealed."

"Like what?"

"I don't know. That's what we've got to figure out."

Mark picked up the composite profiles that the research department at the agency had sent him. "Maybe the answer is here."

Jessica and Mark spent the next two hours going over the files, reading them out loud to one another, to no avail. They separated the biographies into two piles—one containing information on the political wives who couldn't possibly, on the surface anyway, have anything to hide, and another for the rest. "As far as I'm concerned, any one of the women in this stack had the potential to do something reckless—the kind of thing they could later be blackmailed about, or at the very least would not want revealed. And really, all things considered, it's understandable," Jessica murmured, skimming the bio of a woman whose family had been uprooted ten times in the last fifteen years because of her husband. "Who could blame her—" she thumped the photo of the Iowa senator's wife "—for being dissatisfied with her life? Or, if the rumors are true, asking her husband to quit political life after his term? She told us when we talked to her that since moving to Washington she almost never had any time alone with her husband. And their children had even less. The rest of the wives in this stack are in the same boat. They constantly wrestle with the demands of being a political wife. They all have to travel constantly between Washington and their home states. They barely get through one campaign when they're forced to begin worrying about another. In the meantime they have to try and raise their families—often without much help from their husbands."

"Not your idea of an ideal existence, hmm?"

"None of the women even have careers. I mean, how could they? Their time is so divided and given over to the needs and demands of their husbands."

"Life on the periphery," Mark mused. He sighed and got up to fix them both a glass of pineapple juice.

They drank in silence. He looked at her over the rim of his glass. "You don't think it'd be possible to be happy if you were a political wife?"

She shook her head slowly. "I'm too independent. I want things for me, not just for the people I love. I'd never be a good helpmate. I guess I'm too bossy. I like being in charge."

"So do I." Realizing they had that in common, his smile deepened. He took another deep draught of his juice, draining the glass. He set it aside, then dropped onto the sofa beside her, his innate restlessness momentarily tamed as he fanned out the papers like a deck of cards.

Jessica was quiet for a moment. "It says here Pamela Fieldler was very interested in astrology at one time—about six years back—that for a while she even planned her daily activities around the stars."

"Okay, so that links her with the Patty Crowell character in 'Dreams of Glory.'" Mark frowned, staring at the names of the thirty wives in Suzette's journal, contrasting them with the seven characters in her novel. "If only there was some way to narrow this down a little quicker—"

"Maybe there is," Jessica said with sudden inspiration. "Remember how the wives in Suzette's book spent a lot of time at socials?"

"You think we should get ourselves invited to Pamela's group?"

"Maybe it won't be the same group as in the book—"

"But maybe some of the women that Suzette portrays will be. At least it's worth a shot," Mark said.

Using all his considerable charm, Mark managed to get them both invited to the next bridge game, which was being held at Pamela Fieldler's home that very evening. He said they wanted to observe and record a typical recreational evening among the inner circle of wives. No men save Mark were allowed; this was an event strictly for women.

While Jessica busied herself observing and occasionally chatting with one of the wives, Mark took photo after photo.

"How's your new diet coming?" Gloria asked the California representative's wife, as she dealt the cards.

"Great, I've never felt better," said the vivacious woman who was known nationwide for her work on behalf of emotionally disturbed children. "You should all switch to tofu and natural grains instead of that chocolate almond cake you're eating." Jessica smiled, making a note to connect the California woman with the health nut in Suzette's book.

Gloria was obviously the recovering alcoholic Grace, and Pamela the former dancer who struggled constantly to maintain her dancing weight, even going so far as to look to the stars for answers on how to do just that.

Pamela rolled her eyes at the advice. "You'd have to hypnotize me to eat tofu."

"Hey, don't knock hypnotherapy! I've used it to quit smoking," said the Iowa senator's wife.

"I advocate running," chimed in the Mississippi senator's wife, who was well known for her volunteer work at Children's Hospital. "My doctor recommended it as a way to fight stress, and now I'm up to eight miles a day."

Jessica made a mental note to check her later against the compulsive runner in "Dreams of Glory."

"That's what middle age is all about, learning to cope with just about everything," Gloria said with a smile, passing on the cake the maid had offered and asking for a glass of plain tomato juice instead.

When Jessica and Mark left the Fieldlers' home two hours later they were certain they'd identified four of the seven in Suzette's roman à clef. In celebration, they stopped briefly for dinner at the Roof Terrace Restaurant and Hors D'Oeuvrerie at the Kennedy Center for a late supper of burgers and pastries. From their vantage point in a ruby-red banquette, the quiet room looked elegant. Floor-to-ceiling windows afforded them a view of the Lincoln Memorial, while a harp and flute duo provided relaxing entertainment. Replete and weary, they took a taxi back to the hotel.

"Your neck still hurting you?" Mark asked as they entered their suite.

She knew she'd been moving stiffly; she wasn't aware he'd noticed. "That and my shoulder blades," Jessica admitted, knowing it would be useless to pretend otherwise when he was watching her so closely.

"Let me see what I can do for you," Mark said sympathetically.

He helped her remove her coat, watching as she winced at the movement. Earlier Jessica had assured him she didn't need medical treatment, she was just bruised. Now he wasn't so sure.

"Let me look at it," he said, his fingers already nimbly tugging at the hem of her soft turtleneck sweater.

Shy about exposing her body to him, she stubbornly held down the fabric around her waist. "Mark—"

"Come on." He paused at the recalcitrant look on her face. "Your only other choice is the emergency room."

That she didn't want. She'd had enough of hospitals when her mother was dying. Reluctantly Jessica let go of the hem. Gently he edged up the sweater until it was over her breasts. "Well, lady, you've got one hell of a bruise there." His hand caressed her shoulder blade, the nape of her neck. Gently he lifted the fabric a little bit higher. "Looks like a little swelling, too." He turned her around to face him, his eyes dark with concern. "Can you move all right?"

"Fine, I'm just a little stiff. I'm sure nothing's broken."

Her face was bright scarlet.

"Look, let's get this sweater off, then I'll fix you up with a little ice, okay?"

Jessica was too tired to protest. "There's some aspirin in my purse."

"I'll get you some water. But first, the sweater." One by one he extricated her arms, then spread the stretchy collar with his hands until he could get it easily over her head without hurting her neck further. He tossed it aside. She was standing in front of him, in navy lingerie that dipped low between her breasts. Lacy but not transparent, it made the most of her gentle curves. She knew there was no need for her to be so embarrassed; he would have seen as much had she been in a bathing suit. But she was shy just the same, and all too aware of him and his gaze. "I'll get that water, and the ice," he said softly.

He returned with the aspirin and glass of water, acting as if everything were natural. She swallowed the aspirin under his watchful gaze, then handed him the glass. As she did so, their fingers brushed. She felt the minute physical contact as acutely as if she had been singed, and knew from the look on his face that it had been the same for him. They were very close to forgetting caution and making love. All it would take was one more kiss...one more long, sensual embrace....

Unbidden, her mind filled with images of Mark. She sucked in her breath, feeling another charge of electricity ripple through her, turning her insides to liquid.

As if having similar thoughts, he moved restlessly away and suggested abruptly, "Why don't you go in and lie down on the bed? Probably on your stomach would be better."

For a variety of reasons Jessica agreed. She was also, she admitted, more than a little disappointed he hadn't used the opportunity to take her into his arms one more time. But then she knew, as he did, that keeping things platonic between them was best. If only she could stop wanting him so, stop daydreaming, stop...hoping....

He was back seconds later, placing the towel of ice between the nape of her neck and her shoulder. Jessica shuddered at the icy contact. "Cold? I'll get you a blanket." He covered her gently, with warm strong hands. "That better?"

"Much. Thank you." But she still hungered for him.

He cleared his throat and moved restlessly beside her. "I want to take another look at those profiles."

"Okay." She knew she couldn't bear to be this close to him much longer, not if they didn't touch.

Although she had closed her eyes against his magnetic gaze, she could feel his eyes on her face. "Call if you need anything," he insisted.

"I will," she promised.

MARK WENT into the other room, glad of the distance between them. This relationship between them was getting too damned complicated, he thought, stirring up uncomfortable feelings. Whether Jessica realized it or not, she was a small-town girl, who needed the familiar to make her feel safe. He was the kinetic opposite—needing constant change in everything around him. But the attraction they were feeling for one another was stronger than anything he had felt before. He knew, as did she, it wouldn't take much to get them into bed together. And he was afraid that if he did make love to her, he wouldn't be able to leave her. Not the way it was going to be necessary to distance himself from her when this case was wrapped up. Field agents couldn't have families. They were loners, as he had always been. Never before had it bothered him to remain apart from other people. Since he'd known Jessica though, he'd begun to feel his loneliness acutely. Maybe it would disappear when he left her. He hoped so. Because if it didn't . . .

Mark fell asleep, his mind still in turmoil. When he awakened the next morning, stiff and sore from falling asleep on the sofa, Jessica was already up and dressed. Whatever vulnerability she'd felt for him the night before had faded. She was studying the profiles the magazine had provided. "What they've given us isn't nearly enough. I want to go to the library, look up a few more facts before we do any more interviews—go in better prepared this time."

He couldn't dispute the fact it would save time if they knew what to ask. "All right. I'll shower and be right with you."

They were on their way after breakfast. For the next day and a half they were chest deep in old newspaper and magazine articles. The in-depth research frustrated them as much as it helped. Again, they could find nothing that would link the women together. Not in the way Suzette had meant. The only thing they had in common was the fact they were wives of politicians. Beyond that, nothing...

In frustration, Mark suggested they give it a rest. "Look, let's just forget about this for a moment," he said as they left the library, "and go back to interviewing the women one by one."

"Who do you want to start with?"

"Pamela Fieldler. I know we've already talked to her once, but not when she was really open. If there's a chance she's in the mood to talk, or even half as cheerful and outgoing as she was the other night at the bridge party, there's no telling what we might find out."

"All right, let's give her a call and try to set something up."

Unfortunately, Pamela was "not available," her social secretary said. And that was all they could get out of her. They decided to call Gloria Rothschild. Feeling Gloria might be more inclined to confide in a woman, Jessica did the telephoning. "Hi, I've been trying to get ahold of Pamela—" Mark watched as Jessica sucked in her breath and stopped talking. "You're kidding!" she said finally.

"What is it?" Mark asked as soon as Jessica had hung up.

"Gloria told me Pamela was in the hospital! She had knee surgery last night."

"What! Why?" Mark sat forward abruptly.

"Apparently she was out jogging on hard pavement—"

"With a bum knee?" Mark was incredulous.

"I know. It doesn't sound very bright, does it?"

And Pamela was not dumb by any means, Mark thought. "Where is she?"

"Potomac General, but she's not supposed to be having visitors."

That wasn't stopping him. Already grabbing his camera, Mark said, "We'll get in." For a second Jessica remained motionless, looking undecided. "I'm going," Mark said impatiently, his face hard. He did what had to be done and had for years; he wasn't about to start apologizing for it now. "Coming with me?"

Jessica sighed, knowing what they were about to do was probably illegal, if not unethical by journalistic standards, but what choice did they have? They'd be nowhere now if they kept to protocol. Besides, Jessica wanted answers as badly as Mark. "After what just happened to her? You couldn't keep me away."

Chapter Fifteen

"Well, here goes nothing," Jessica said as she and Mark sauntered down the corridor toward Pamela Fieldler's private room. "Think she's going to be angry at us for just barging in like this?"

He shrugged and gestured to the flowers he carried in his hand. "There's only one way to find out—"

Pamela was sitting up in bed, her bandaged leg elevated. Seeing Mark and Jessica sneak into her room unannounced, she looked surprised, then delighted—like a mischievous child who'd managed to avoid curfew despite all precautions.

The private nurse in the corner got to her feet, a disapproving look on her face. "Mrs. Fieldler isn't receiving visitors."

"Mrs. Fieldler is," Pamela corrected her. She gave the nurse a withering look. "I want some time alone with my friends. If you'll excuse us—"

"The senator won't like this."

Pamela smoothed the bobbed ends of her dark hair and turned irate cornflower-blue eyes on the woman in white. "I don't give a hoot what the senator likes or doesn't. I want to be alone with my friends." The nurse remained motionless. "It's either leave or get fired," Pamela threatened direly. The nurse left.

Pamela rolled her eyes and gestured for Mark and Jessica to have a seat. She looked extraordinarily well, Jessica thought, considering she'd just had knee surgery the previous day.

"We weren't sure you'd want to see us," Jessica began.

Pamela smiled, her eyes dancing with devilish lights. "I'm glad you came. I've been dying with boredom."

"You're not supposed to have visitors?" Jessica asked.

"They want me to rest. Fat chance of that! I sit here, looking out the window, feeling like I'm going out of my mind." She shook off her bleak mood and looked at Mark. "So how'd you hear?"

"We talked to Gloria."

Pamela grinned at the mention of her closest friend. "She's been sneaking in to see me, too. Of course, she's on the list of approved visitors."

"How did it happen?" Mark asked.

Pamela flushed with embarrassment. "It was the stupidest thing, really. I was out jogging." She shook her head again, as if that would clear it. "I was on hard pavement." She held up a cautioning hand. "Don't say it. I know better than to run on something like that with my bum knee."

"Then why did you?" Mark asked, grinning, in a way that made the question curious rather than rude.

Pamela was charmed and answered, "I guess I just wasn't thinking. I've had a lot on my mind lately." She shrugged, as if that were the end of it.

Jessica tried hard to keep her shocked feelings to herself. "Are you in a lot of pain?"

Pamela adjusted the high-collared, embroidered bed jacket around her throat. "I guess that's debatable. It doesn't hurt as much as it did when I was in the car wreck that ended my dancing career. But maybe that's because I don't have nearly as much to lose now by becoming immobile—" she grinned like a teenager who'd just found the perfect excuse to get out of doing the dishes "—except maybe to miss out on a few political luncheons." Changing gear once again, she looked over at the vase Mark had put on the dresser. "The flowers are lovely. Thank you for bringing them."

Mark smiled back. "We wanted to cheer you up."

"You have." Indeed, Pamela looked as if she felt better already. "So what have you two been up to? How's the work going on the profiles?"

They had no chance to answer. At that moment, the door swung open again and Gloria Rothschild and Dr. Conti walked in. They looked surprised to see Mark and Jessica there. "We were just leaving," Mark said.

"Don't go," Pamela said, holding out a beseeching hand. She glanced imploringly at them, signaling that she really wanted them to stay. "The two of you can hear anything Gloria and Dr. Conti have to say."

Dr. Conti looked reluctant to proceed. Gloria wasn't so easily intimidated. "You know why I'm here. I want you to think about seeing Ethan."

"Professionally?" Pamela scoffed. She seemed agitated.

"Or we can talk as friends," Dr. Conti suggested in a soothing you-can-tell-me-anything voice. "I just want you to know I'm here to listen."

Pamela stared at his lean, aristocratic face and suddenly became hostile—not just to Dr. Conti, but to everyone in the room, especially Gloria. "You think I'm

crazy, don't you?'' Pamela shouted. ''Well, I'm not!''
She looked at Mark and Jessica, as if begging them for
support. ''Do I seem crazy to you?''

Before either Mark or Jessica could answer, Gloria
intervened. ''Pamela, don't do this to yourself. Please,
hon. Please just let me help you. I can see what you've
been going through and I'm worried about you.''

Gloria's kindness was apparently more than Pamela
could bear. Abruptly she began to weep in great,
wrenching sobs.

Jessica felt worried and uncomfortable. She mo-
tioned to Mark who stood watching. As discreetly as
possible, they took their leave.

Dr. Conti followed them out into the hall. ''I trust this
display of Pamela's won't end up in your book?''

Jessica could see he really cared that Pamela not be
depicted as a neurotic fool. ''Of course not,'' Jessica
said. ''We don't want to see her hurt. She's a lovely
woman.''

''A bit impulsive maybe,'' Mark said with a frown.

''She's going through a rough time in her life. I have
every confidence she'll pull herself together again,'' Dr.
Conti continued, ''with the help of her friends.''

''Do you fall into that category?'' Jessica asked. He
had seemed more familiar to Pamela than she would
have expected.

''I know her through the Rothschilds. We've attended some of the same parties. The senator, as you
know, has been instrumental in helping provide more
money for mental health counseling for the poor.''

Jessica and Mark were silent. Behind them they could
still hear Pamela weeping, and Gloria's soothing voice
as she attempted to comfort her friend. Jessica knew it
was rude to ask, but couldn't help it. ''Do you think

Pamela will go into therapy?'' From her erratic behavior there appeared to be no doubt that she needed something.

Dr. Conti was quiet for a moment. As the sounds of Pamela's sobbing rose, so did his visible concern for the troubled woman. ''I don't know. Right now—like most people—she sees just asking for help as a sign of deficiency on her part. If she gets past that, I know she would benefit from therapy.''

Before they could continue, the nurse was back. Walking beside her was Senator Fieldler. His expression was set and angry. ''Conti, what the hell—'' he began furiously. ''Who told you Pamela was here?''

''Gloria.''

''I don't want you around my wife!''

The nurse went into the room and Gloria came out. ''It's time she saw someone professionally,'' she said coolly.

Senator Fieldler turned on her wrathfully. ''Who in blazes' name are you to judge? Pamela's not the one who's a lush, Gloria. You are. So if you need help, you get it for yourself. My wife doesn't need a shrink!''

Gloria recoiled as if the senator had slapped her. ''At least let her get away for a few days. I have a friend who's got a place in the country—''

''Absolutely out of the question. Pamela has duties here. Yes, she's embarrassed about the accident with her knee. She's hated physical infirmities all her life. But that doesn't mean I'm going to allow her to wallow in self-pity. She has responsibilities here, to others and to me, not just to herself. I'm going to see she meets those responsibilities.''

''At whose cost?'' Gloria hit back.

"I really don't think—" Senator Fieldler inclined his head toward Mark and Jessica who were still lingering in the background. He pointed a finger at the pair. "I'm warning you. One word of this leaks to the papers, and I'll know where it came from. I'll sue the pants off you."

Jessica believed him. But it wasn't his threat that would keep Mark and herself quiet, it was what such a disclosure would do to his wife. "I'm not in the business of hurting people unnecessarily," she said smoothly. Turning on her heel, she walked out. Mark caught up with her and wrapped a protective arm around her waist.

"YOU HANDLED YOURSELF just fine in there," Mark said as they left the hospital.

"Thanks. So did you. What do you think about Pamela?"

"I don't know. Could be she's having a nervous breakdown. It wouldn't really surprise me. Political wives are under enormous stress. For all her bravura in public, she seems a little more fragile than the others."

"I used to think the same about Gloria, but she certainly seemed strong today."

"She knows Pamela needs her. Love can be a powerful well to draw from."

Jessica knew that. There wasn't much she wouldn't have done for Suzette—or Mark, although they were fast becoming more than simple friends.

He spied a pay phone. "I want to call in, see if Noah's uncovered anything on his end. Do you mind?"

"Not a bit."

He returned to her side several minutes later. "I've got some information on Tamara North. Apparently she was about to be sued for libel on another tell-all book. My editor at the magazine says the parties involved are really going for blood. They're asking fifty million settlement, ten of which were to come from Tamara's literary agency."

"That would ruin her."

"Bennett was threatening her because of Suzette's activities, too."

"Two lawsuits of that nature in a single year would ruin her business."

Jessica was quiet. "Well, that explains why she was so uneasy when I talked to her."

Sticking to their plan, Mark and Jessica spent the rest of the day interviewing the remaining political wives. By evening, they thought they had made yet another link— between a Georgia representative's wife and a character in Suzette's book—both of whom were talented artists, avid Agatha Christie fans and reformed chocaholics.

Encouraged by their progress, they were nonetheless more than ready for a break from their grueling research. They might be able to find a pattern; though having the final portion of Suzette's book would help immensely. "Why don't we just drop it for a while? Go out tonight and have dinner?" he suggested amiably, as they left the last house and headed back in the direction of their hotel.

The idea of dining alone with him in some place cozy and romantic did have its appeal. She also knew it was dangerous. She told herself she could handle the experience, as well as her feelings for him. "Martin's Tavern isn't very far from here. It's just a block or so over on Wisconsin."

"You know the place?" He seemed pleased they had that in common.

"Suzette and I used to go there, when I'd come to DC to visit her." Suzette had liked both the atmosphere and the fact that it was always filled with jocks.

"It's a favorite place of mine, too. I'm crazy about their crab cakes and corn chowder."

"Their bluefish meunière isn't bad, either."

An hour later, replete after a good dinner and a shared bottle of white wine, they lingered over coffee and dessert. "You know, after this is wrapped up, you don't have to go back to Ohio," Mark observed. "You could get a job in New York."

And be near him—but what if their romance didn't work out? New York City seemed so big and impersonal, and that scared her.

"You think that's a very risky move, don't you?" he asked gently.

The corners of her mouth curved up wryly. "And you don't understand why I'm so conservative."

"I'd like to."

His low intimate tone sent shivers down her spine. Her fingertips grazed his. It was one of the few times she'd touched him without being coaxed. "I guess it goes back to my roots. You would have to understand how it was for me, growing up."

"Tell me about it," he directed quietly, his eyes on her face, his voice so gentle and filled with understanding that it made her want to cry.

She took a deep breath and heard her voice shake. "It wasn't an easy life. Money was very tight. My mother worked as a receptionist in a law office and also delivered papers every morning at 5:00 a.m. I used to go with her and toss them out the car. I'd help her mail out the monthly envelopes. When I could drive, I took over the paper route altogether."

His hand covered hers completely, infusing her with warmth. "It sounds tough."

"It was, but we had each other." She turned her hand under his so their palms met. "And we were happy. But that happiness was found only by keeping within strict financial limits."

"How did she feel about you being a writer?"

She drew her hand from his to reach for her glass. "To be honest, I think she would've preferred to see me enter a more lucrative field. You know, something with more job stability and security. But she was proud of me, too. Every time I won some award for my writing—I even got a couple of college scholarships because of my essay writing—she would just beam. And in the end I knew she was happy for me. I knew she believed I would succeed. And while I was trying to make it, I always had the house. You see, the cost of living in Spring Valley is very low—especially when compared to the East Coast or the big city. And a writer can write anywhere."

"But by being on the coast or in New York you'd make invaluable contacts. I could introduce you around to some of the editors—"

She toyed with the stem of her glass. "You could still do that for me if I made a trip to the coast once or twice a year." And it would be so much less of a risk.

"Yes, I could, but it wouldn't be the same as having you living there with me." He cupped her chin, then leaned across the table to kiss her lightly. "I'm getting used to having you around."

She felt a wild thrill at his admission and uttered a gentle sigh.

A smile still on his face, Mark paid the check, and they walked out into the dark city night. *Eight-thirty.* There was still a lot of traffic in Georgetown. A chill wind had blown up, it was snowing lightly again, and they huddled together in front of the crosswalk, straining toward the curb, eager to be in his car and on their way back to the hotel.

Later, she was never sure how it happened. One minute they were standing together, watching the traffic whiz by as the last of the cars going north south tried to beat the light, the next they were being shoved forward, knocked off balance and into the street.

Hands out in front of her, Jessica hit the pavement. Bystanders screamed and the crowd parted hysterically as a taxi screeched to a halt just inches from her outstretched fingers. Mark landed beside her with a thud, he too only narrowly missing being run over. Swear words hissed through his teeth. Jessica found she was cursing, too, adrenaline pulsing through her veins. Pausing only to make sure she was okay, Mark was up and running. Jessica took some steps to follow but knew she couldn't keep up with him. In the distance, through the haze of falling snow, she could see a running figure in black. Jessica was unable to make out whether the person was male or female, but did have a faint impression that whoever had pushed them was favoring his or her right ankle slightly.

Mark picked up speed. Seconds later, Jessica lost him completely. She paused, leaning against a store window, her sides aching, completely out of breath, aware there were tears of terror and frustration on her face. When Mark rejoined her several minutes later, his face was a mask of anger. He swore again. "I lost him," he said grimly, searching her face. He took her into his arms, his embrace strong and warm and reassuring. "Are you all right?" he whispered, holding her close.

Jessica nodded. *For now.* She wondered, given the circumstances, how long it would be so. For now, there was no doubt. Someone was trying to kill them both. And if they didn't soon discover who it was, the killer would try again. And the next time he or she just might succeed.

Chapter Sixteen

"Amazing, isn't it, that Pamela'd be back on the DC social circuit so soon?" Jessica murmured two days later to Mark as he snapped several photos of the congressional wives.

"You heard her husband at the hospital. She has obligations to fulfill. Though judging from the way it looks, the partying isn't doing her any harm." On designer crutches, she looked spectacular.

"I'm going to go say hello," Jessica said. "Lovely luncheon, isn't it?" Jessica began mundanely, slipping into the seat next to Pamela's.

"Yes, I really adore seafood," Pamela said.

Jessica paused. They'd had chicken *cordon bleu* for the main course. She laughed uneasily, figuring it was a joke. "So how's your knee?"

"Oh, the usual postoperative problems. Swelling, pain..."

Maybe painkillers were the reason for the vague, spacey look in her eyes, Jessica thought. Something wasn't right here—unless it was just the strain of being out in public again after so short a recovery period. "Did they give you something for that?"

Pamela shrugged. "Aspirin."

Jessica noticed Pamela was drinking mineral water, nothing stronger. "Mark and I would like to spend some more time with you, to continue our work on the book." Since her accident, they'd discovered they wanted to know much more about Pamela—like why she had dived into that swimming pool at a recent party. Of course, it was possible she'd done so merely to humiliate her husband—to ruin his career, the way he had ruined Pamela's in that auto accident years ago. Yet for all her foibles, Pamela didn't seem the vindictive type. *Mischievious, yes. Deliberately hurtful, no.*

Pamela looked at Jessica and smiled, once again seeming all there. "I'd like to meet with you again. And I'm very pleased you're including me in the book. A positive portrait of me will bolster my husband's image, you know, and in turn that will positively affect his career."

Suddenly she seemed so concerned about the senator. Jessica puzzled over it, wondering what had brought about the change of heart. Had he threatened her with divorce?

Jessica had no more opportunity to question her, for several other wives came up to them. She went to rejoin Mark. He was standing off to one side, reloading his camera. "What's wrong?" he asked under his breath.

It was both gratifying and disturbing to have him read her moods so easily. Briefly Jessica explained about Pamela, ending with the worry that she might be having an adverse reaction to painkilling drugs.

"I don't think so. Her pupils weren't dilated when I photographed her. It could be the continuation of a breakdown, though. She seems in some way out of sync."

To their chagrin, Pamela left the gathering minutes later, begging off because of her knee. Although Gloria offered to take her home in the Rothschild limousine, Pamela insisted on taking a cab.

The meeting broke up soon afterward. Mark gathered up his equipment and ushered Jessica to his rental car.

They had only gone about four blocks from the hotel where the luncheon had been held, when they hit upon a giant traffic jam. Emergency vehicles zoomed past, their sirens screaming. Mark pulled over and parked at the curb. Grabbing his camera, he leaped out of the car. "I'm going to see what's happened."

She knew his interest wasn't ghoulish, that he was simply doing his job. Not wanting to be left behind, she followed.

To their horror, it was a very bad accident.

A cab had swung around sideways and smashed into a street cleaning truck. The cabdriver had come out of it almost unscathed, with only a few minor contusions, which the emergency people were already treating. His passenger had not been so lucky. A blanket covered the form that lay in the street. Even from a distance they could make out the distraught words of the cabdriver. Hysterical, he was sobbing, "It wasn't my fault, I tell you! The crazy broad...she started screaming and screaming, said I was gonna wreck. I told her I wasn't gonna wreck, but she wouldn't shut up. The screams!" He covered his ears in anguish, just remembering. "Youda thought she was being mugged or something."

"Just calm down and tell us what happened next," the cop said, watching as the medical services technician applied direct pressure to the cut on the driver's cheek.

"I tried to pull over. I was moving in behind that truck when—still screaming her head off—the broad opens the door and starts to jump out! In the middle of traffic even! I hit the brakes, tried to stop, you know. I swear to ya, I didn't want her to get hurt."

"And that's when she fell out of the cab?" the cop asked, writing furiously as witnesses lined up to collaborate the cabbie's story.

"Jumped out is more like it." The cabdriver shuddered, recalling. "Although how she did it with that bum knee of hers—"

The cop looked over her shoulder at the technician who was leaning over the shrouded body, turning back the blanket. "Any identification on her?" she asked.

But for Jessica and Mark there was no need to identify the dead woman. They already knew, even before they saw her scraped face. The dead woman was Pamela Fieldler.

"I DON'T BELIEVE she committed suicide, as the early television reports are hinting," Jessica said, shuddering as she swiftly downed the brandy Mark had given her.

Equally upset by what had happened, he paced their hotel room. "I don't want to accept that explanation, either. It seems implausible. But we have to face facts. She was alone in that cab. There are a dozen witnesses who can attest to the fact. No one forced her to open the door, and all the witnesses said the cabbie didn't do anything to prompt her action—certainly not in heavy traffic, at that speed."

"But why? Why would she start screaming? I know she was under a lot of stress lately, with the trouble between her and her husband, her knee injury and the pressure to get back into the limelight again so soon."

"Maybe whatever drugs she was taking for her depression, combined with alcohol she maybe drank surreptitiously at the luncheon, reacted to cause delusions of some sort. Maybe she was afraid they were going to have a car wreck—irrationally afraid. After all, she had been badly hurt in a wreck once before. Maybe she was afraid it was going to happen again."

"It wasn't the first time she'd acted erratically, though. She took a dive into a swimming pool fully clothed a few weeks ago." Jessica and Mark hadn't been there, but everyone in Washington had heard about it.

"Maybe it was the drugs then, too. They were serving alcohol at that party, and from all reports she was drinking that night—"

"I guess you're right." Jessica was silent. "She was behaving weirdly at that luncheon. Mark, one minute she'd seem fine, and the next she wouldn't make any sense. I'd look into her eyes and it would be like looking at a stranger." Jessica wished she'd known, or could somehow have foreseen the tragedy, so she could have prevented it. But she knew even as she thought it that that was just wishful thinking. No one could have known. No one.

"Gloria must be beside herself," Jessica murmured, recalling how close the two women had been—as close as Suzette and herself.

NOT SURPRISINGLY, Gloria was not at her best at the funeral. Mark had been assigned to cover the service for *Personalities*, and Jessica went with him.

The first opportunity she had, she went to Gloria's side. "I'm sorry," she said, taking the older woman's hand.

Tears poured down Gloria's face. Knowing Jessica was someone she could confide in and trust not to betray her, Gloria said, "I just don't understand it, any of it. Sure, Pamela's been increasingly unpredictable over the years, but she would never have committed suicide, never. Not on her own, anyway. Not unless someone was—"

"Gloria! Darling! There you are!" Douglas Rothschild suddenly materialized. Taking his wife gently by the arm, he murmured soothingly, "Darling, you've been through a lot. Let me help you to the car."

Craig was there, too, his face tearstained and white. "Mom, let me help you," he said, moving to flank her other side.

Shut out, Jessica stepped back. Bennett walked up to join her. A short distance away, Mark was snapping photo after photo of the mourners. "You've turned into a real vulture, haven't you, Jessica?" Bennett accused her grimly. His eyes hardened. "Just like Suzette."

Jessica swallowed, seeing the anger in his eyes. "That's not true—" she said around the tight knot in her throat.

"Isn't it?" Bennett murmured. Apparently he had his doubts. And suddenly so did she. Wasn't she acting now the same way Mark had acted at Suzette's funeral?

Recoiling at the realization, Jessica moved away from Bennett.

Beyond them she saw Senator Rothschild with his arm around the grieving Senator Fieldler. Rothschild seemed in full command of the situation and was leading the other man to the waiting limousine. Broken and sobbing, Fieldler hardly seemed to know what was going on.

Mark walked up to join her. This time, as if realizing the grief was too raw and too private, he didn't snap any photos, though other photographers on the scene weren't so principled.

"A hell of a shame, isn't it?" Mark commented between grimly compressed lips.

Jessica thought of Pamela. Refreshingly candid, mischievous, a woman who'd danced to her own beat, they would all miss her. "A hell of a shame," she concurred sadly.

Try as she might, she couldn't shake the feeling that Suzette's story was somehow connected.

"THE FUNERAL really got to you, didn't it?" Mark observed softly, hours later when they were alone again in the hotel suite. She looked away from him, hoping he wouldn't notice her trembling mouth and her stupid babyish behavior. A warm wash of color filled her pale cheeks.

"Yeah, it did," she began in a low monotone, embarrassed. His eyes were on hers, curious and compassionate, urging her to continue until she'd told him all the deepest secrets of her soul. "I keep thinking about her family, all her friends. I know how it hurts to lose someone you love." And she knew how it felt to love—to wonder if that feeling would ever be returned.

"You're thinking of Suzette, too."

She nodded, realizing he'd made the same connection she had made at the graveyard. "And my mother." She gulped her brandy, barely noticing the burn of the alcohol as it slid down her throat. "I don't know what it is about funerals, but every time you go to one, you think of the rest you've been to."

He seemed determined not to let her get by with a glib remark or change the subject. "You miss her?"

The catch in her throat intensified until she could barely swallow. "More than I can say." Jessica briefly let herself drift with the memories. "Always a parent, sometimes a friend. I—" Her eyes filled with tears, and she had to struggle to go on. "I guess I really never thought I'd lose her, certainly not as soon as I did." Jessica gulped hard and continued, wanting him to understand. "Even when she was diagnosed with cancer, I didn't have any idea. I wouldn't admit—"

"Denial's natural, so is grieving."

"I know." Furious with herself for the display of self-pity, she brushed away her tears with the back of her hand. "I don't know why this is hitting me so hard, tonight of all nights. After all, it's been almost a year since my mother died. It's not as if it happened suddenly, either. I had time to say goodbye—the chance to tell her how much I loved her—" Without warning, tears were streaming down her face, and she longed for the comfort of her mother's arms.

What she got was Mark's arms around her, strong and secure, holding her tight. He stroked her hair and she let the tears come, let them flow until she was exhausted and limp. "It was probably seeing Pamela's children at the graveside that did it," he said. "They're all in college, not much younger than you. It'd be strange if you hadn't identified with them."

"You make it all sound so logical," she murmured against his damp shirtfront. He made her feel so safe.

"I'm sorry you're hurting," he said, his voice tender and caring against her hair. "I'm so sorry."

She nodded, and arms laced around his shoulders, continued to hold him tight. She needed his touch, his strength. But it was more than that. "You know how I feel."

He pulled back. "Feeling better?"

She nodded. The crying had helped. So had his embrace. "I just needed to be held," she whispered.

His eyes darkened, his expression revealing how vulnerable he was, too. Suddenly she knew they'd come to a crossroads of sorts. A decision had to be made. Her heart slammed against her ribs, and tension wracked her slender frame. She felt hot and cold at the same time, and knew that if she had any sense of self-preservation at all, she'd get the hell out of there now before it was too late.

But she couldn't leave. And maybe she'd known from the start that once involved with him, however timorously at first, that she never would be able to turn and go—not without at least experiencing love with him.

He raised his head to look down at her. His breath was hot and sweet on her upturned face, his expression implacable, as if he had read her mind yet again. "Is that all you need?" he asked warily, telling her that he wanted more, not just for himself, but for both of them.

She caught her breath as a new thrill chased over her skin. *No.* His holding her wasn't all she needed. With the emptying of her grief had come a certain peace within her, and with that the freedom to feel again. And what she felt at that moment was a love for Mark that was stronger and fiercer than anything she had ever imagined. Complications aside, they were now connected in ways that would never end.

He felt her tremble and tightened his grip. "Jessica," he said softly.

At the yearning in his tone, the last of her doubts fled. She saw him hesitate to take advantage of her in this state. But the time for hesitation was past.

"Mark, I—" *I want you, I love you.*

"I know," he murmured when she couldn't finish. He threaded his hands through her hair, arranging the strands like threads of silk. "I'm feeling it, too." Then his mouth was on hers. He kissed her slowly, dreamily, searching for everything she felt, all she had to give. She glowed with pleasure, the kind that could last for hours. Lacing her arms about his neck, she stood on tiptoe, leaning into him. He stroked her soothingly, his touch a balm to her ravaged nerves. When her mouth warmed and softened under his, he deepened his kiss and felt her shudder.

Together they found the bed, undressing as they went. A dreamy interlude enveloped them, then he took her places she'd never been before, showing her every shading, every nuance, until there was nothing else, only the two of them, only love.

Chapter Seventeen

The phone rang at 5:00 a.m., jarring Mark and Jessica from a sound sleep. Because she was closer, Jessica grabbed the receiver and dragged it to her ear. "H'lo."

"Jessica—Jessica, you've got to help me!" a woman cried plaintively at the other end.

Reminded of a similar call she'd received from Suzette, Jessica bolted upright. "Who is this?" she demanded. Already her hands were trembling. Alert to the tone of Jessica's voice, Mark sat up abruptly and dragged a hand through his hair.

"It's Gloria! My husband is trying to kill me! He—he made me come to this place again, and he knows I hate it out here. They keep forcing those treatments on me, and I'm frightened!" Her voice caught on a hysterical sob.

"Where are you?" Jessica snapped, already pushing her legs over the side of the bed. "Mark and I will come and get you."

"I'm—" the line seemed to fade "—out of town!"

"*Where?*" Jessica asked desperately. Gloria was so hysterical that she wasn't making any sense. "You've got to tell me where—"

"I'm in the bedroom!" Gloria interrupted, screaming again in terror above the thunderous racket in the background. "I barricaded the door with a chair, but it isn't going to hold for long!" In the background there was a loud crash, then Jessica heard the muffled sound of a man yelling, and Gloria screamed. The line went dead.

Jessica felt waves of shock and fear engulf her.

"What's up?" Mark demanded, noting the alarm in Jessica's face and voice. He was already pulling on his pants and shirt, and was reaching for his shoes.

"Gloria Rothschild," she said, trembling. She repeated the whole conversation, then paused, musing. "Do you think she's at the same mansion Suzette referred to in her journal, wherever that is?"

"Must be," Mark said briskly, angry and impatient. Both knew there was only one person who would know where that was—the person who'd put her there—the senator.

It took them ten minutes and innumerable broken traffic laws to reach the Rothschild town house in Georgetown. To Jessica's dismay, the house was dark and silent. Taking the front steps three at a time, Mark rang the bell. And then rang it again. And again.

The senator appeared several minutes later. In bathrobe, pajamas and slippers, his hair rumpled from sleep, he was irate. "What the hell do you think you're doing? Do you have any idea what time it is?"

Mark shouldered his way past. "We just had a call from your wife. Where is she? What have you done with her?"

The senator looked startled, confused. "I don't know what you're talking about. Clearly this is one of Gloria's childish pranks. She often pulls them when she drinks. There's even a term for it, I believe—alcoholic-induced delusions."

Similar to what had killed Pamela? Jessica wondered.

"She didn't sound that way to me," Jessica said.

"That's part of the problem. She never does—right up until the time when she passes out." The senator sighed.

"Then where is she?"

"I put her on the plane for Dallas late yesterday afternoon. She was supposed to go to the Golden Pavilion Health Spa for a few days of rest and relaxation. After Pamela's death, she felt she needed it. Considering all she's been through, it's not surprising she would be drinking."

Mark stared at him. Jessica knew how he felt. She was damned if she could tell whether or not Senator Rothschild was lying. He looked sincere—yet politicians were notoriously good at turning the tables and slipping out of sticky situations unscathed. And he'd been running around with other women for years. In fact, had he not seduced Suzette, Jessica doubted she would ever have discovered what a two-faced character he was.

"And the doctor?" Jessica demanded coolly, wanting him to explain that, too.

The senator shrugged. "Maybe she is with a doctor. I'm not familiar with the specifics of the spa's staff. Satisfied?" Now the senator looked tired—almost as if he realized for the first time what his wife had put them through. Suddenly Jessica wondered if maybe it *was* Gloria who had the problem. Maybe the senator was only trying to cope as best he could with a difficult, potentially explosive situation, one that if disclosed could spell the end of his political career—or at least his ambition to become president.

Mark faced the senator impatiently. "You do believe we had a call from your wife?"

"Yes, although I have my doubts about whether or not she was in danger. It's not the first time she's been hysterical—all this is off the record, by the way. Print one word of it, and I'll sue you for defamation of character. Say what you want about me, but I won't have my wife maligned in print."

"You needn't worry about that," Mark muttered between tightly gritted teeth. "I'm not in the business of ruining people for sport." He paused again, stymied. "We need to talk to your wife. So if you could get her on the phone—"

Reluctantly the senator went to the hall phone and dialed information. Seconds later, the operator had connected him to the Golden Pavilion. The senator requested to speak to his wife. As he listened, his face grew ashen. "What do you mean, she never checked in?" His tone and manner became frantic. "Dammit, I put her on a plane myself! I know wealthy women often change their minds! No!" He calmed slightly. "Yes. I know you're not responsible. I'm sorry if it seemed that way—"

Minutes later he hung up, soaked with perspiration, his face still gray. "She's gone," he said quietly, already dialing the police. He swore again, mumbling a prayer for her safety, a curse at her drinking. "I don't know how I'm ever going to forgive myself, if something has happened to her!"

THE POLICE showed up minutes later. Normally it would take twenty-four hours before a missing persons search could begin. But because Gloria was the wife of a United

States senator, the rules were bent. Jessica and Mark repeated their story.

"Was the call long-distance?" the police officer asked.

"She said she was out of town." Jessica looked at Mark. "The connection was poor once or twice, but that may have been more due to the snowstorm that's been brewing rather than to distance."

The senator groaned, then muttered, as if to himself, "She could be on another lark."

"Well, wherever she was," Jessica said, "she wasn't alone. I could hear a man in the background yelling at her and pounding on the door." She glanced at the senator. He still looked ashen. Where was Gloria? Was she all right? Was this really just another of her drinking binges? Was she with a lover, perhaps? Was she in danger? Or had that person only been trying to get into the room to keep Gloria from doing herself harm or drinking any more? And what about the senator? Was he lying to them, pretending not to know where his wife was?

"Maybe you should call your wife's doctor, see if he's heard from her," Jessica suggested.

The senator nodded dutifully. "Perhaps you're right." Unfortunately, their family physician had not heard from Gloria at all. Nor did he like the way things sounded.

"It'll take us several days to access the telephone company computers and trace the point of origin of the call," the police officer advised them. "In the meantime, we'll put equipment on your phone, Senator, in case she calls you."

"Thank you. Of course, I want this kept quiet."

"We understand. We'll do our best."

Jessica and Mark started to leave.

"What do you think?" she asked when they reached the curb.

"I don't know. Within the Company—" slang for the CIA "—Gloria has long been considered a security risk. She's not responsible for her actions, not in the least."

"Pamela was her closest friend here. I don't know who else she would turn to."

"The senator didn't seem to know, either."

"And if she wasn't with her family doctor—"

"The only doctor I've seen her with in recent weeks is Ethan Conti."

"Let's call him." They stopped at a pay phone. Mark stepped inside the booth, while Jessica waited in the car.

His face was pale when he returned. "You're not going to believe this," he began. "I talked to Conti's service. Apparently he's out of town for a few days—at his estate in rural Virginia."

"Rural Virginia!"

"I know. I didn't like the sound of that, either." Could Conti's country home possibly be the mansion Suzette had alluded to in her book, the secret place where the wives went to relax and unwind? Was Gloria there? Did her husband know? And if she was, was Conti caring for her as a friend, or trying to treat her? Jessica knew Gloria needed help. But from the way she'd sounded on the phone, whatever help she was getting was not necessarily the kind she needed.

Her heart pounding with trepidation, Jessica asked, "Did you get a phone number where he can be reached?"

"Yes, but the lines are down. Apparently they had one helluva snowstorm overnight, knocked out all the telephone lines about half an hour ago. The operator said it'll be hours before they can get through again.''

Jessica's mouth was dry. "Mark, you don't think— could Gloria be there? Could she have called just before the lines went down?'' Was that the reason they'd been disconnected so abruptly?

He started the engine, a determined look on his face. "There's only one way to find out.''

CRAIG ROTHSCHILD relaxed in the big soft bed, floating gently in that hazy stage between wakefulness and sleep. He wanted to open his eyes, but couldn't; he was too tired, too...happy just the way he was. Although he knew what he would see if he did open his eyes—a large blue room in a cozy hideaway. Luxurious, spacious, it had everything a nineteen-year-old could want. Stereo, TV, video and computer games. To date, he hadn't used much of the electronic equipment at all, he realized lazily. *No.* To date, he had mostly eaten and slept and eaten and slept some more. There'd been the tapes, of course, the endless listening to the music he most enjoyed, and in between his albums by Whitesnake and Joshua and UB2 and Bryan Adams, sometimes he listened to those instructional tapes his host favored.

He grinned, thinking of the stupidity of the messages on them. What did the man think he was? Retarded? Or just ripe for those self-motivational spiels?—how to be a better person, how to be a better student, how to decide upon a life career, how to make yourself happy or allow yourself to love, to find that lasting relationship with a woman. A woman suitable for marriage.

Craig frowned. Suzette would not have been that, not in anyone's eyes, but Craig had loved her all the same. Even though she'd slept with his father. She hadn't thought he had known, not for a long, long time. And when he had finally confronted her with the truth, things had gotten ugly, so ugly.

She'd said she never wanted to be bothered by him again. He'd said "Good." And then the next thing he had known, someone was telling him she was dead. Dead. Suzette.

Tears began slipping down Craig's face. He missed her. He wanted her alive. He didn't understand why she'd had to die. Or why she'd slept with his father rather than himself.

She'd wanted a glimpse of the fast track, she'd said. Hadn't Craig given her that? Hadn't he tried to give her everything? Why had she betrayed him?

Chapter Eighteen

It was still snowing five hours later when Mark and Jessica arrived at Dr. Conti's Virginia estate. The roads had been treacherous. They'd run into the snowstorm just west of Manassas, and had continued to battle it all the way to Lynchburg and deep into Campbell County, where Conti's home was located. It had been an arduous journey—even in the four-wheel-drive Bronco Mark had managed to rent. "I can see why someone would want to come here. It is beautiful out here," Jessica said as they drove slowly through the front gateway of the large estate. Drifting snow covered the rolling pastureland and draped the trees. The house was a sprawling two-story Colonial mansion built of gray stone and trimmed in white and dark pine green. It was elegant and old—maybe a century or so.

"And very secluded," Mark murmured as he parked in front of the house.

Dr. Conti greeted them at the door. Clearly not overjoyed to see them there, he nonetheless ushered them into his front hall. "I can see you're very worried about Gloria," Dr. Conti began when they'd told him their story. He paused, giving the impression that he was wrestling with the question of medical ethics versus compassion. Apparently compassion won out. He sighed heavily. "Normally I couldn't say anything. But since Gloria's already involved you—"

"What happened last night?" Jessica asked.

Conti wanted to make a bad situation good. "Senator Rothschild knew Gloria was operating under a tremendous strain. He felt she needed to get away— completely away. He suggested she go to the Golden Pavilion for a few days. Gloria had always liked it there before. She agreed, but then as she was getting ready to go, she found a woman's perfumed handkerchief among her husband's possessions. She didn't recognize the initials on it. Shaken and angry, she called me and said she needed to get away for a few days. I was already planning to come down here, so I readily agreed."

"Is this routine for you?" Mark interrupted him.

Conti seemed to take offense at the slightly interrogative note underlying Mark's voice. "Yes, as a matter of fact it is. I have a number of patients who're very high profile. When they need to get away and simultaneously need some counseling, I offer them refuge here. Right now I have another guest here, too. In warmer weather the rooms are filled. Anyway, the sobbing you heard was due to her hallucinating about someone wanting to harm her. I discovered a half-empty bottle of vodka later."

"Did Senator Rothschild know at this point where she was?"

"No. She didn't want me to call him. She said she needed a few days to herself, to sort things out, and didn't want to explain to him why she'd canceled her original plans. I could see there was no way of convincing her otherwise. So I planned to let it go until this morning and try to talk her into contacting him, or at least into letting me tell him where she was."

"And did she agree?"

"Yes, but by then the phone lines were already down." He paused, studying them both. "I can see you're worried," he said once more. "Would you like to see for yourself that she's all right? It might even do her good to see the two of you. She must feel she can depend on you, or she wouldn't have called you last night, even in her agitated state."

Mark and Jessica exchanged glances. "We'd like that very much."

DR. CONTI LED THEM into a paneled den where a fire blazed in the hearth. Gloria was sitting at a desk, writing busily. Dressed in a skirt, sweater and silk blouse, she looked chic and composed, if a bit pale and chalky. But then, what could one expect after all she'd been through recently? Jessica thought. It was amazing to see her so composed now. Only seven hours before, she'd been hysterical.

"Hello! What a surprise!" Gloria glanced at Jessica and Mark and smiled.

"How are you feeling?" Dr. Conti asked gently, looking pleased but not surprised to see Gloria so chipper.

"Much better! Although I still feel as if I could sleep for a week!" She put down her pen and smiled again, expectantly this time.

"We don't want to interrupt—" Jessica said. Whatever Gloria had been writing had seemed engrossing.

"That's all right. It's just personal notes—to some of our constituents back in Ohio." She sighed, a hand to her throat. "I'm ashamed to admit how I've lost touch with some of our old friends. I wanted to catch up on my correspondence, but that can wait." She looked again at Mark and Jessica. "What have the two of you been up to?"

What had happened to her anger at her husband? Jessica wondered. "We've been worried about you," Jessica said slowly.

"Oh." Gloria sobered. "Because of Suzette's death, I know. It was quite a shock for all of us, but now that the funeral is over—"

Mark and Jessica exchanged a glance. Conti was equally wary, though clearly not quite as dumbfounded. "Actually, we were thinking about Pamela—" Mark cut in.

Gloria's gaze widened artlessly. "What about her?"

She really doesn't know, Jessica thought, briefly shocked into speechlessness. *She doesn't remember her friend's death.*

Before they could answer, Conti stepped between Mark and Jessica and stayed them with a light touch on the arm. "I promised to show you the house," he said easily, evidencing great charm. Beneath the surface pleasantries, Jessica could see his mouth had tightened—with worry? "Gloria, would you like to come, or would you rather finish your correspondence?"

"I'll stay." She smiled serenely, the perfect Washington wife, then picked up the pen again and began scribbling, as if she hadn't a care in the world.

Jessica stared at her a second longer. What in the world was wrong with Gloria now?

"Obviously she's had a blackout and doesn't remember either Pamela's death or the funeral," Dr. Conti murmured as soon as they were out of earshot.

"Shouldn't we tell her?"

He frowned, appearing to consider the question. "No, not at this point. Once she's a bit more rested—"

Jessica couldn't deny Gloria was exhausted, there were bluish circles under her eyes that not even the best cosmetics could hide. She seemed to be operating on the edge between madness and sanity. Conti was the psychiatrist; he obviously knew best.

"At least she's not drinking this morning," Mark muttered.

"Yes, I can shield her from that. Temporarily, anyway," Dr. Conti said. He led them into his private den and from there around to the dining hall and into the warm, cozy kitchen, where he introduced them to his housekeeper, a retired nurse. A pleasant, mild-mannered woman, Mrs. Logan looked to be in her late fifties.

"You are staying for lunch, aren't you?" Mrs. Logan asked. Looking outside at the snow that was still falling, she shivered.

In contrast, the atmosphere inside the large country kitchen was incredibly inviting. A hearty stew was simmering on the range, bread was baking in the oven. A homemade apple pie, steam still rising from the slits in the center, lay cooling on the counter.

Mark's stomach growled. Jessica was suddenly aware it had been hours since they'd eaten.

"Yes, please do stay," Dr. Conti said somewhat reluctantly after a moment, his tone stiff but pleasant. "The company will do Gloria good."

Mark and Jessica were of one mind. They both wanted to see more of Gloria, have time to observe her. "You've convinced us," they said in unison.

While Mark went off with Dr. Conti to view his coin and stamp collections, Jessica returned to visit with

Gloria. Still looking enviably serene, she cut right to the heart of the matter as she poured them both some tea. "You really were worried about me, weren't you?" she murmured.

She obviously had no recollection of her hysterical phone call and apparent hallucinations. "Yes, I was," Jessica said simply, admitting, "It was a relief to me to find you looking so well." Especially after all she had been through. "Dr. Conti is a good friend to you, I gather."

"Yes, we've known each other for years. His wife Barbara was a friend of mine."

Jessica hadn't realized he was married. "Does she live here with the doctor?"

Gloria shook her head, "No, his wife died ten years ago, shortly after his son."

"I'm sorry. I didn't know—"

"Poor Ethan. Their son Christopher was everything to them. Their whole world revolved around him, but when he drowned in a freak accident at summer camp— everything fell apart. The children were playing some underwater game during free time, and he either hit his head or got a cramp. Nobody really knows, but by the time they found him it was too late."

"Dr. and Mrs. Conti must have been devastated," Jessica murmured compassionately.

Gloria nodded reflectively. "I think it was hardest on Barbara, though. You see, it had been Barbara's idea to send him to camp. She worried about him living out here on the farm, not having other children to play with."

"Did Dr. Conti—Ethan—blame her, too?"

"No. As heartbroken as he was, he knew it was just a freak accident, and that it wouldn't do any good to assign blame. But Barbara just couldn't get over it, and she killed herself about two months later."

"I had no idea," Jessica said, touched by the tragic story.

"Yes, well, although Ethan doesn't try to keep it a secret, he doesn't dwell on it, either. I know he wouldn't mind if you knew. Besides, it's a matter of public record. But he has had a hard time of it himself. That's why I feel so comfortable with him, I think. Because I know he does understand what it is to feel stressed-out and alone."

"Are you thinking of entering therapy?" Jessica inquired.

"Ethan wants me to start seeing someone regularly, but I don't know." She looked down and sighed, as if his judgment meant a lot to her. "If I were to see anyone, I'd want to see him."

"Wouldn't your friendship get in the way of that?"

Gloria frowned, but didn't reply.

"So how are you two ladies doing?" Conti asked, as he and Mark joined them once again. "Anybody hungry? Mrs. Logan tells me lunch's ready, whenever we are."

Mark looked at Jessica. "We'd better eat if we hope to get back to Washington tonight."

"Yes, considering the fact it's still snowing, the sooner you get on your way again, the better," Conti agreed. He couldn't have been more obvious, had he tried to push them out the door. He couldn't wait to get rid of them, Jessica mused.

Chapter Nineteen

During lunch, Mark sat next to Jessica, his senses acutely attuned to everything going on around him. Something wasn't right here. He'd known it almost as soon as they'd arrived. Gloria was too calm, too serene. Everything was just a bit too cozy, Conti just a bit too cooperative. He wasn't sure yet what was going on, but he knew something was. "Have you heard from Craig?" he asked Gloria.

"Oh, he's fine. He loves school." Gloria fanned her face with her open palm, as if feeling suddenly warm. She smiled at Ethan. "Darling, be a dear and get me some wine. I think a nice Bordeaux would go nicely with the stew—"

Conti's mouth tightened disapprovingly. "Gloria—"

"Now, don't nag, Douglas," she said. "It isn't nice."

Douglas? Mark thought. *Douglas?*

Recovering his poise, Dr. Conti smiled nervously at Gloria, then sent Jessica and Mark a questioning glance, to indicate he was as much in the dark as they about what was happening with Gloria.

Sensing Gloria's impatience, Conti turned back to her. "I don't think we have any wine," he said.

"Of course we do. Here, I'll get it!" Before anyone could interrupt, Gloria tossed down her napkin and went to the wine cellar behind the kitchen.

"Is she having a nervous breakdown?" Jessica whispered, leaning forward anxiously.

Conti looked reluctant to commit himself to a diagnosis.

Gloria returned, jauntily waving a bottle of Bordeaux. "Ethan, be a darling and open this."

She called him Ethan this time, Mark noticed.

Conti looked to the two of them for help. "I really don't want any wine," Jessica said.

"Neither do I," Mark added.

"Nonsense. A meal without wine is a meal without sunshine." She glanced impatiently at Ethan. "Douglas, darling, I want some wine. And I want it now, please."

The steel magnolia lives, and she's just called Ethan "Douglas,"—her husband's name—again, Mark thought.

He expected Conti to argue with her, plead, remind her of her alcoholism. Instead he did neither, simply pouring her a very small amount. Mark frowned. He wouldn't have expected Conti—a psychiatrist—to give in to her weakness. But then there was a lot they didn't know about the man and his connection to the Rothschild family.

Jessica had turned very pale. He knew how she felt. He felt as if he were trapped in a real-life horror show, too—or at the least a very sudsy drama.

Gloria sipped her wine, then lifted her glass. "I propose a toast." She looked at Ethan. "To your reelection, darling."

Not knowing what else to do, Jessica lifted her glass. So did Conti. Reluctantly, Mark complied. He gave Conti a disapproving look. Conti sent him one back that said *What the hell else do you expect me to do?*

"Cheers," Gloria said, tapping the rim of her glass against the three others.

"Cheers." The sentiment was echoed lamely.

Jessica faked cheerfulness and dug into the savory stew. "So, how's life at the magazine, Mark?"

Mark dutifully answered Jessica, rambling on and on while watching Gloria. She'd already downed one glass and had started on a second. Although only two minutes had passed, if that, she was already visibly affected. Her eyelids were dropping. Suddenly she looked as if she was having trouble staying awake. Without warning, her sweater sleeve dipped into the gravy.

"Uh—Gloria—" Pointing, Jessica alerted her to the clumsiness.

Gloria mumbled agitatedly and sat back in her chair.

No doubt about it. She needed help, Mark could see. He leaped up and grabbing her arm from beneath, came to her rescue. "Here, allow me," he said.

Jessica's face whitened with the strain of having to pretend normalcy in such a bizarre situation. She handed him her cloth napkin.

Dr. Conti rose, his unhappiness evident. "I'll go get a damp cloth from Mrs. Logan."

Gloria began to cry. "Oh my God, my sweater! It's cashmere. It'll never come out."

Mark had to admit the stain didn't look promising. He dabbed ineffectually at the gravy, then cushioned her weight when she slumped against him. Unbuttoning her blouse at the wrist, he lifted the sleeve, dabbing at the sodden mess from underneath. As he did so, the silk fabric slid upward, revealing needle marks at various places from midforearm to elbow. *Heroin?* he wondered. Gloria? Had the connection to Vinnie the pusher been through her? Was it possible Craig—or Suzette—had been buying drugs for her? Or had Suzette figured out the real root of Gloria's problem—maybe Pamela's too? Had Pamela been tripping out on acid when she threw herself from that cab?

Hastily he replaced the sleeve. Gloria did not appear to have noticed what Mark had seen. He breathed a silent sigh of relief. Domestic dramas weren't his thing, but he also realized the agency—the CIA—had every right to be concerned. Gloria, because of her husband's position, could be at the center of one hell of a mess.

Suddenly Mark had the feeling he was being watched—and not by anyone he might consider friendly. He glanced up casually to see Conti standing in the doorway with his housekeeper behind him. *He knows,* Mark thought. *He knows about the drugs.* Mark gave him a guileless smile. "Uh . . . Gloria doesn't seem to be feeling too well."

Conti's gaze narrowed. "I'm not surprised. She hasn't had a lot of sleep." Then to Gloria, more gently, "That wine hit you very hard, didn't it?"

"Yes," Gloria murmured sleepily. She yawned around her hand. ". . . so tired."

"I think we'd better put her to bed," Conti said, setting the damp cloth aside. "Mrs. Logan, perhaps you could give me a hand."

Looking troubled about Gloria's behavior but not surprised, Mrs. Logan nodded.

"Is there anything I can do?" Mark asked.

"Just finish your meal," Dr. Conti directed calmly. "And I'll be back down to join you in a minute." He gave Mark another hard warning look. "We'll talk then. I promise."

As soon as they'd left the room, Jessica was at Mark's side. "What's going on?" she whispered insistently. She knew from the look on his face that he had discovered something ugly.

Briefly he told her about the needle tracks on Gloria's arm.

"Oh, no!" Jessica exclaimed, slumping against him.

"It's all right." Mark's arms went around her.

"Maybe we should get out of here," she whispered, holding onto him. "And just take Gloria with us, even if we have to do so forcibly. Clearly the woman needs to go to a hospital."

Mark glanced out the window; the snow was still coming down. "We will get her out of here, the first opportunity we get," Mark promised. But first he wanted a chance to look around.

Conti returned, his expression unutterably grim. "You might as well know. I'm having her admitted to a rehabilitation center tomorrow morning. Considering her addiction to both alcohol and drugs, it's the only thing we can do, and I'm sure her husband will agree, once I can get through to him."

"The phone lines are still down?" Mark asked.

"Yes." Conti gave them each a hard look, transmitting his dislike of journalists. "Gloria's hospitalization is going to be kept very quiet. Nothing is to get into the papers. For that reason, I can't tell you where she will be staying, only that she will be getting help, and I can only tell you that because of what you've seen this afternoon. Had Gloria not involved the two of you previously—"

They got the message.

Nonetheless, Mark had to ask. "When did you find out about the drugs?"

"Recently. Yesterday. I guessed substance abuse but I had no idea—I thought it was just the alcohol—until last night."

"And Pamela Fieldler?" Jessica inquired.

Dr. Conti sighed. "I'm really not at liberty to say."

"Off the record," Mark pressed.

"If you don't tell us, we'll just investigate on our own," Jessica continued. "If you do, it doesn't mean we'll print it." In fact, Mark thought, he knew Jessica wouldn't—she was that kind of person. She went out of her way not to hurt others.

"The same." Conti was quiet for a moment or two. Abruptly he pushed away from the table. "Coffee'll be in the drawing room. After that, I'm going to have to ask you to leave."

"I'm sorry, Doctor. We'd like to be out of your way, believe me, but with the roads the way they are—we barely got here in the first place," Mark said. "I think we're going to have to stay, at least until it stops snowing. That shouldn't be for a few more hours yet."

Dr. Conti stared at Mark, anger blazing in his eyes. "This is most inconvenient, you understand."

Mark did, only too well. "We have no choice," he countered firmly.

The other man simply nodded, then noticed that the fire in the drawing room was dwindling. With a baleful eye at the weather, he slipped into a coat, hat and boots and went out to get more wood. Jessica was at Mark's side almost instantly. "Why did you say we couldn't leave?" she demanded.

He could tell that for her the charm of sleuthing had worn off.

His eyes were hard. "Because I want to have a look around."

"Mark—"

"Just go with the flow, follow my lead. It'll be all right." He tucked an arm around her. "I promise." He didn't intend them to stay long, just long enough.

She studied him intently; it did something to his insides to see she could read him when no one else had ever been able to. "You're keeping something from me," she murmured.

Only about a thousand and one suspicions, he reflected, suspicions that came directly from his training days with The Company. But since Conti knew nothing of his real background or profession, Mark had nothing to worry about.

"Just be charming, okay? And try to relax." Unfortunately, Jessica showed her emotions with chameleon-like accuracy, and he didn't want her giving anything away. So for now, for her own safety, he would have to keep her in the dark. Later...later he would tell her everything, including what was in his heart.

In the meantime they had to see this through.

MARK GAVE HER a brief hug, then prowled the drawing room, paying particular attention to the gun cabinet in the corner. Jessica watched him move about with easy grace. The yearning in her welled up once more. How had she fallen for him so hard and so fast? And what would she do when this nightmare ended and she had to go back to living a normal life, back to living alone?

Feeling restless because she had no answers, Jessica wandered to the window. Outside, she saw Dr. Conti

competently loading pieces of firewood into a canvas
sling. As he started back, he seemed to be struggling
under the heavy load. Jessica was about to insist Mark
go out and help, when she noticed he seemed to be
limping slightly, favoring his right ankle.

*The man who had pushed Mark and herself into the
traffic had favored his right ankle.* Her heart began to
pound.

Conti came back indoors, stopping to brush off the
snow before entering the room. He wasn't limping now,
Jessica noticed.

"Well, it's getting lighter; the snow's tapering off."
Ethan Conti dumped logs onto the stone next to the
fireplace. He grimaced again. "Looks like you might get
free before dinner. Well, I've got about two hours of
paperwork to do. If you need me, I'll be in my den. You
might want to rest up before your long journey home."
His meaning was clear.

"That's fine with us." Mark laced a comforting arm
around Jessica's shoulders and pulled her against him.
"I am tired, and I know Jessica is. We drove all night."
Jessica managed to keep a pleasant expression on her
face, but inside she was wondering what was going on.

"No problem," Dr. Conti said tightly. "I'll just tell
Mrs. Logan to get the rooms ready."

"Oh, one room will be fine," Mark said genially, in-
dicating with a smile he knew the doctor understood.
"Won't it, Jessica?"

Jessica nodded and turned to Mark, giving him a
warning look only he could see. She was already planning how she would spend the time—by giving him hell
for manipulating things.

"Right," Conti said, a knowing expression on his
face.

Jessica turned to Mark the moment Conti started down the hall toward the oak doors of his den. He disappeared inside, and Jessica thought she heard a bolt drawn on the door. Her expression was livid as she turned to Mark. "Two seconds to explain, or I take your head off," she threatened.

Chapter Twenty

"You're sure this leads somewhere?" Jessica asked nervously as Mark fiddled with the locked door at the end of the hall. She'd calmed down as soon as she'd learned he'd planned to use their time together to explore. They wouldn't be bothered, he said, during the two hours Conti would be locked in his den. That was good, because Jessica wasn't at all sure they'd get another chance. She felt Conti wanted them out by five o'clock, whether the snow had stopped or not.

"Positive. I think there's a whole wing behind it. You can tell by the architecture we saw when we were driving up." Under his deft ministrations the lock gave, and the door quietly swung open.

Beyond was a dimly lighted corridor. The way it had been shut off, Jessica expected the wing to be cold, dusty, unused. Instead, it was warmly heated and scrupulously clean.

"Come on." Closing the door behind them, Mark relocked it from the other side. He clasped Jessica's hand in his left, while keeping his right hand on the gun inside his blazer.

Her heart tripping along at manic speed, Jessica tip-toed to the first door. They peered in. It looked like a lab in any doctor's office, complete with microscope and various machines. "What do you think he's doing here?" Jessica whispered.

Mark shook his head silently and tightened his grip on her hand. "We'll know soon enough," he whispered back.

They continued down the corridor. The next door was locked. Mark picked it, too. As they opened the door, they heard soft music playing in the background. In the center of the room was a large antique bed. Craig Rothschild was lying on his back, sleeping peacefully.

"My God, what's he doing here?"

"Maybe this is the isolated retreat they were talking about."

"Do you think he's getting psychiatric help?"

As they moved closer to the bed, they stopped talking completely. Barely audible above the strains of the music was a taped message, urging Craig to become the good student and loving son he was capable of being.

Jessica grew pale as she saw the needle marks on Craig's arms. There must have been ten or twenty.

Mark led her out of the room.

"They're brainwashing him, aren't they?" Jessica had to fight to contain her horror and keep her voice down.

Mark nodded. "That kind of depatterning went out years ago, because it never worked. Damn Conti! He must think he's some sort of wunderkind." His hand still on his gun, he urged Jessica on down the corridor. "C'mon," he whispered. "Let's see what else we can find."

The next room had more machines, computers—and an examining table fitted with broad leather restraining straps. Just looking at it gave Jessica the willies. "Electroshock therapy," he said, his expression growing even grimmer.

Jessica shuddered and stayed close to his side. "I read about that when I was in college. Patients who've been put through that suffer memory loss and confusion, don't they?"

Mark nodded. "Which explains Gloria's confusion earlier—assuming Conti's been shocking her, and I think he probably has." There were several more rooms down the corridor, including one that had enough drugs in it to rival a pharmacy.

Jessica felt ill. "I've seen enough," she murmured. "Let's get out of here." She was so scared that she was shaking.

Mark looked physically steady but equally upset. "I'm with you. I've seen about all I can stomach, too."

"Let's get Gloria and—what's this door?" Jessica turned a questioning look on him.

"I don't know," Mark murmured, noticing the door was not wooden, but metal. He ran his hands around the frame, checking for wires. "It looks like some kind of simple vault."

While Jessica nervously kept watch, Mark turned the metal handle. The door swung open, revealing a large room roughly the size of a walk-in closet. Inside stood a file cabinet, assorted tape recorders, an inventory of cassette tapes—and two American Tourister suitcases Jessica recognized. "Those belonged to Suzette!"

Inside were the last pages of "Dreams of Glory," along with the many notes she'd made over the years.

Mark and Jessica eagerly divided the pages, quickly skimming them for content.

Neither liked what they found. Mark handed her a passage.

The more Daisy thought about it, the more she considered experimenting with drugs. She told herself it was only to see what others got out of them, to understand what a real high was. But when she examined her real motives, as her shrink had taught her, she knew it went deeper than that. She was looking for an escape, an easy way out. Why? Because she was afraid. Afraid of her own ambition. Afraid of what her snooping would turn up.... So Daisy began going to the sleazy pusher, once a week at first, then more often. It was difficult. The pusher rarely told her what she wanted to know. Instead, he sold her lots of Valium, which Daisy used occasionally to calm her nerves. But she drew the line at the harder drugs like angel dust and acid and coke. She still wanted to know what the drugs did to you, how they made you feel or behave. She wasn't willing to use herself as a guinea pig to find out.

"Well, I guess that tells us *her* death wasn't a suicide," Mark said.

Jessica handed him a few pages she'd earmarked as important. "But she did come to a very important conclusion about Grace—or Gloria."

Mark began to read aloud. Daisy was finally beginning to put the pieces together, to understand how

Grace could be so unhappy one minute, then so dazzlingly content the next.

At first she was puzzled, because Grace would disappear for two to three days at a time, then reappear looking wonderfully rested and fulfilled. The aura would usually last three or four weeks before it began to wear off. Wanting to know why, Daisy began to follow her to the rendezvous.

And there the real horror started. Grace's miraculous transformation was due to a psychiatrist, who saw not only Grace at his secluded Virginia estate but a number of other political wives, as well. He seemed able to program them any way he wanted, turning them into health nuts, compulsive runners or nonsmokers. Daisy was fairly sure the women were being drugged, perhaps even hypnotized in an effort to make them perfect political wives.

She wasn't sure how involved the husbands were in these treatments.

"I don't know about you, but I want to look at these files," Mark said.

Swiftly he and Jessica began rifling through them. They found Conti had been seeing, as Suzette had suspected, several wives they had identified in Suzette's book, plus several more. The California representative's wife, the Iowa senator's wife, the Mississippi senator's wife.

Conti's notes on some of the files indicated he felt he had succeeded magnificently. "Look at this," Jessica whispered in awe. "He even told them what charities to work on—"

"After first getting input from their husbands," Mark whispered back, appalled. "The man's a monster."

"So the husbands must have colluded—" Jessica began.

Without warning there was a click on the other side of the door. Jessica and Mark rushed toward it, but the heavy metal door wouldn't budge. Mark swore luridly, a look of desperation on his face. "We're locked in."

Immediately Jessica began to panic. She'd always hated small places; they made her claustrophobic. "We've got to get out of here," she whispered frantically.

"I know." Mark's expression was grim.

"Because if Conti's leaving—"

"Chances are we wouldn't be found for days, if ever." And there was no way they could survive in the small locked chamber without food or water.

Mark looked at the door. No lock was visible. It would take a blowtorch to get them out of there. "We're really stuck, aren't we," Jessica murmured, a lump of terror in her throat.

Mark was silent, frowning, his hands balled into fists at his sides. Suddenly to Jessica it felt unbearably warm. She moved around restlessly, and it was then she looked up, spying the metal grille above them. "Mark, there's a vent!" she whispered hoarsely.

He nodded, having already noticed it, and went back to reexamine the door. "I know, but it's too small for me to get through." His shoulders alone would never fit.

"I can do it."

Mark glanced at Jessica, then at the vent, which couldn't have been more than fifteen inches wide and of about equal length. He started to shake his head, his masculine protectiveness coming through loud and clear. "Jessica—"

"Lift me up. I mean it! I think I can squeeze through! Lift me up!"

He stared at her, sternly considering. "You could get stuck. At best it would be a very tight fit."

"It's our only chance."

Mark was fuming like a volcano about to flow. "All right," he said finally, through clenched teeth, agreeing her idea was the only viable option they had. "But if you do make it, get to the lock to free me right away. I don't want you alone with Conti longer than necessary. And if you can't figure out the lock, here—" he thrust the keys to the Bronco in her hand "—just get the hell out of here and go for help. Understand?" He stared at her tensely, his features set in granite.

Jessica nodded and threw herself into his arms. She hugged him fiercely without saying a word, but there were tears in her eyes when he released her. Wordlessly Mark wove his fingers together and made a foothold. Jessica stepped into it, and he lifted her. Using her fingers, she pulled down the grating. Inside, the vent was black as night. When she put her hands up, she encountered layers of filth and something that felt crunchy and hard, like a dead bug. She shut her eyes, shuddering involuntarily.

Noticing her hesitation, Mark changed his mind about letting her go it alone and said, "Jessica—"

Determinedly she swallowed the revulsion in her throat. What were a few crawly things, if she could get out of this alive? "I'm going. Now push me up." Angry with herself for her show of cowardice, she pulled herself up and in. Getting her shoulders through the opening was a tight squeeze, but somehow she managed to wiggle in.

That was the easy part. Forcing herself to continue in the inky darkness, without so much as a flashlight to lead her way, was another matter entirely. Gritting her teeth, she moved blindly along the tunnel, the thin metal creaking beneath her. Finally she came to a juncture. Trying to decide which way to go, she finally went right. Another fifteen feet and she passed the next room. Looking down through the metal slats of the air vent, she saw the bedroom was empty. Without warning, Jessica's hands began to perspire. She had no idea where the room lay, or where Conti was. She only knew she had to get out of that air vent. Forcing open the grille from behind, she pushed until it came loose, barely managing to hold on to it as it broke free. With slippery fingers, she worked it backward and to one side. *Now the hard part,* she thought. *Getting down into the room without making a sound.*

Deciding to go feet first, she scooted forward, all too aware of the tremendous roaring in her ears and the dizzying pace of her heart. There was a tense moment when she wedged her hips in the hole, but pushing hard, she managed to work herself out. With a sprinkling of plaster, she fell out. Unfortunately, her tenuous physical control lapsed at that point. Her hands slipping as she hit the edge, she landed on the carpeted floor with a soft thud. Jessica lay there for a moment, her heart pounding, the metallic taste of fear in her throat. Ear to the floor, she listened hard for the first sound of someone coming. *Nothing.*

She sighed her relief. She was safe. For now.

Slowly, her arms and legs shaking badly, Jessica got to her feet. She reached into her pants pocket and felt for the keys to the Bronco, curling her hand around the reassuring metal. Mark had said, *If all else fails, go for help.* But she had no intention of leaving him here, within range of Conti. Somehow she would find a way to free Mark.

But where was she?

Moving like a wraith, Jessica opened the bedroom door and slipped out into the hallway. Cautiously she looked both ways. *Nothing.* Soundlessly she started down the hall, all too aware her heart had never pounded quite that frantically before. Amazingly enough, she had a clear path down the stairs. The drawing room was equally empty. The draperies were closed, the fire in the grate was out. Sheets draped some of the furniture. Jessica picked up the phone hopefully, but to her disappointment it was still dead.

Moving swiftly to the gun cabinet, Jessica selected a lightweight rifle, hoping she wouldn't have to use it. She had it in hand when an imperious voice sounded behind her. "Put it down."

She turned to see Ethan Conti facing her. He was warmly dressed in cords, boots and a heavy sweater. He had a small pistol in one hand, a suitcase in another. "You'll be dead before you even figure out how to get the safety off!" He stepped toward her, his face blotchy with fury. She heard him cock his revolver, saw the intention on his face, and knew she had no choice. Her brain might be telling her to run, but her gut instinct said she should stay rooted and surrender the weapon.

Swallowing hard, she leaned forward and put the gun down. Where was Mrs. Logan? Had she left? For the first time she noticed how utterly silent the house was.

Conti waved his gun at her, jerkily motioning her away from the cabinet and the rifle. Jessica moved slowly, anxiety and desperation washing over her in numbing waves. Advancing on her steadily, he pushed her into a corner. Momentarily satisfied, he paused, the gun still trained on her, his chest heaving. "You stupid snoop, you're just like your friend Suzette. You just had to keep pushing, didn't you?" Conti snarled angrily, closing in, his own frustration apparent.

Jessica knew the time for running had passed. Her only choice now was to flee and get shot in the back, or try and stall him, persuade him that it was in his best interest to let her live. But first she had to stall. "You were the one in Suzette's apartment that night, weren't you?" Her chin angrily rose.

"I had no choice but to kill her! She broke into my office."

That's it, Jessica, keep him talking. "Because she knew about Gloria and Pamela and the others?" Jessica questioned calmly, as if they had all the time in the world.

"I didn't want to kill anyone." He fingered the trigger. She saw madness in his eyes as his voice softened pleadingly. "I only wanted to help."

"Oh, I've seen how you help people, by brainwashing them!"

He mopped his face with his handkerchief. "Don't blame this all on me! What's going to happen to you now isn't my fault! I tried to warn you, to scare you off.

To let you know what would happen if you persisted in this investigation—''

Jessica felt the blood leave her face. "Then it was you who burglarized my home in Ohio!"

"I had to find out how much you knew."

"And right now you're brainwashing Gloria and Craig—''

"Whenever possible, yes, if that's what it takes to make them happy!" He moved closer, waving his gun in emphasis and sneering at her. "Regular therapy doesn't do a damn in some cases! If it did, my wife would be alive!"

Suddenly it all fell together for her. Conti thought he was doing a public service for them; he thought he was saving lives. His own tragedy was the driving force behind his madness. That meant the politicians did not know the truth. Senator Rothschild had no idea his wife was getting electroshock and chemical treatments for her condition.

Her legs felt unsteady as the horror penetrated. She knew chances were she'd never be able to reason with him. The only thing she could do was keep him talking. "But Pamela committed suicide—" she whispered harshly.

"So the therapy didn't work for her either—" He looked frustrated.

He was still three feet away and sweating profusely. Desperate, Jessica determined to keep him talking. "Did you kill Vinnie, too?"

Conti nodded. "The little weasel was blackmailing me, because I bought the street drugs from him that killed Suzette."

"Why is Craig here? Whose idea was that?"

Conti looked impressed. "You got around, didn't you? The senator's, of course. That boy of his is far too easily led. He knows I can help. I helped his wife. I'm sure he'll be a model son, now that he's been guided to apply his energies in the right direction."

"You did that to the women, too, I suppose?" Jessica remembered the audio tapes she and Mark had uncovered in the vault; she could guess at their content.

His jaw hardened stubbornly. "They need to make their husbands happy."

Hence Gloria diligently writing letters to her husband's constituents. "Only some went too far," Jessica continued. "Like Pamela, who was so concerned about keeping her shape that she dived into a swimming pool during a party and jogged on a weak knee—"

"She was difficult," Conti admitted openly, with the scientific air he might use to study rats in a cage. "Resistant, hard to program. And then when she did have a success, she'd have a memory loss or faulty logic. It upset her to wake up in strange hotels and not remember where she'd been or with whom."

The man was truly evil, Jessica thought. "She told you that?"

He nodded, looking and feeling omnipotent. "She thought she was with another man."

"But it had been her husband—" Abruptly Jessica felt ill again.

Conti shrugged. "I let her believe it, because the guilt worked at keeping her in line."

Jessica remembered seeing Senator Rothschild comforting Senator Fiedler after his wife's funeral. *"You've got nothing to blame yourself for,"* he had said. *"You'd done all you could and then some to help her."*

The men didn't know, did they?'' she questioned angrily.

"No. And they still won't after I've finished with you."

Behind them, footsteps sounded on the parquet floor. "Ethan! Darling, there you are!" Gloria started into the drawing room, only to stop dead in her tracks as she saw the gun in Conti's hand. "Ethan!" She sucked in her breath, confused.

"Gloria, go back upstairs," Dr. Conti ordered harshly. "I'll come for you as soon as we're ready to leave."

He wasn't the only one who was feeling jumpy, Jessica thought. Her knees were knocking so hard that they were banging together almost painfully.

As she took in the scene before her, Gloria's face grew white. "Douglas, what are you doing?" she demanded slowly. "What is going on here?"

From the second floor came the sound of a metallic banging and a muted pounding. *Mark,* Jessica thought. *He's trying to get free.*

Conti swore. He looked at Jessica, his expression grim, telling her in no uncertain terms her time was up. "I didn't want to have to do this here, but you've left me no choice. Let's go!" Swiftly closing the distance between them, he grabbed her by the arm and jerked her around, poking the gun into her back.

"Where are we going?" Jessica tried unsuccessfully to get away.

"To the basement." He held on fast, digging his fingers painfully into her arm.

He was going to kill her there. "No," Jessica said, stopping dead in her tracks and refusing to move, her fear engulfing her until she could no longer breathe. "No!"

From behind them, Gloria's voice sounded hysterical. "Ethan, let her go. I mean it, or I'll shoot. I won't let you kill her. She's my friend." Beneath the raw emotion was a lethal calmness that made Jessica's hair stand on end.

Conti swallowed hard, lessening his grip slightly. "Gloria, put the gun down!"

But Gloria had cocked it and fired wildly. The gun went off, the bullet slamming into Conti's shoulder. The impact thrust him backward against the wall, and when he landed he lay eerily still.

Chapter Twenty-One

"They're going to have a cover-up—the president's orders," Mark informed Jessica later the following day. It had been an exhausting twenty-four hours, with endless questions to be answered by both of them, and official reports to be filed by Mark. But now finally they were together again—at least for the moment, Jessica thought, watching as he sank onto the hotel sofa beside her. She was acutely aware that their hours together were about over.

"He's been informed?"

Mark nodded, capturing her hand. "Because of the women involved, the families, they felt he had to know."

He watched her steadily, this time as one journalist to another. "How do you feel about that?"

"Good as a person, bad as a journalist. You've got to admit it's one incredible story." She shook her head and sighed, visualizing the splash it would have made. Gloria had been admitted to a real psychiatric hospital; so had Craig and Audrey. The other political wives who'd been "treated" by Conti would also be receiving legitimate help over the next few months. Mrs. Logan, his housekeeper, had been taken into custody. Gloria had not been arrested for Conti's death, because she hadn't been in her right mind when she pulled the trigger, due to Conti's "treatments." The coroner had also decided the gunshot wound alone would not have killed him; the head injury had spelled his doom.

"What's going to happen to the husbands? Are we sure they know what Conti was doing to their wives?" Jessica asked.

Mark nodded. "Yes. We're sure. They thought the therapy was legitimate. They knew the women came back well rested and happy after a stay at the farm. It never lasted, but…they were grateful for whatever peace they found."

"Noah told me the agency is going to pay you for time on this project," Mark added, gently stroking her arm.

Jessica nodded. "Yes, Noah's been very nice about that." She grinned wryly. "Which is good, because I probably won't get my job back at the paper, since I still can't explain what I've really been doing the past couple of weeks or why. But they tell me I can free-lance those profiles on political wives, although I'll be severely restricted as to what I can write about them."

"What the heck. It's a start in the big time, right?"

They were both silent. Jessica was aware there was so much she wanted, and that it was as always just out of her reach. She knew one thing for sure. She'd never loved a man the way she loved Mark, and never would again.

Mark sighed reflectively and leaned back against the cushions, stretching out his long legs in front of him. "I'm sorry you were put through this, Jessica. If I'd had any idea how dangerous it was—but I didn't—and by the time I realized, you were already in too deep. You were safer with me. So I had to keep you with me."

She'd wanted to be with him. "That's all right. I would've looked for the truth with or without you."

He gazed at her steadily. "So when are you going back to Ohio?"

She couldn't tell what he was feeling. Oh, she knew he cared about her—as a friend. But friendship wasn't really what she wanted from him. Not when for one glorious moment in time they'd been everything to one another.

She got up, blinking hard and glancing out the window, determined not to let herself shed so much as a single tear. They'd had too much that was good for her to ruin it now. Deliberately she focused on the sunshine. Already the snow was melting. It was remarkable how quickly things changed. And suddenly she knew she couldn't bear to let the goodbyes drag out any longer. They'd been together, it had been wonderful while it lasted, but Mark had warned her he was a man with a notoriously short attention span. She didn't want to hold him down.

"I'm on the evening flight out."

Jessica saw a quick flash of reluctance on his face, then the acceptance she now felt herself. After all, they were both adults. They knew this was coming. "I'll call you about the series. We've already got most of the photographs—"

"And the other interviews can be conducted either by phone or in person. I know you're busy. You won't have to tag along for that," she said. She didn't think she would be able to bear it.

"All right, if that's the way you want it." He was perfectly amenable.

Her heart aching, she said it was.

"YOU'VE GOT your house up for sale," Mark remarked two weeks later, stopping by unexpectedly.

Jessica opened the screen door and let him in, aware that just seeing him again was making her heart pound and her spirits soar. She had missed him so much. The February air was brisk, but the sky was clear, the landscape glittering with sunshine.

"And you're looking well." His cheeks were red with the cold, his eyes bright and assessing. Unthinkingly she moved into his arms for a quick genial hug—the kind old friends exchange. He held her against him a second longer than necessary, and she felt the flame that had never died dance to new life.

Reluctantly he dropped his arm and stepped back. "I should look good." He grinned. "I've done nothing but take it easy."

She could imagine that—he was the type who eventually played as hard as he worked. "You earned the rest."

"Now you sound just like Noah." His voice was soft and affectionate; it did peculiar things to her insides. "So how's life in the small town?" he asked casually, taking off his coat. He dropped it over a nearby chair and sat down on the sofa, stretching his legs in front of him. "Seen much of Bennett Agee?" While waiting for her reply he looked around, already restless.

"We had dinner," Jessica admitted. But it hadn't been the same.

"The two of you are still friends?"

She nodded, remembering how awkward it had been, how tame compared to the time she had spent with Mark. As soon as the thought occurred to her, she banished it from her mind. Would she forever be comparing all the men she knew to Mark? And if so, how could she ever hope to even date again without somehow feeling cheated? Aware Mark was watching her, she answered his question. "I think it will take him a while to forgive me for holding so much back from him. But we've been friends a long time, and I think he treasures that." He also knew now that she didn't love him, and he'd come to accept it.

"Did Bennett know what Conti was up to?"

"No, and he still doesn't, not really. He just knows the therapy wasn't medically sound. He did know about Suzette's book and tried to stop it to protect the senator, but that was all." And he'd never know the rest. With Conti had gone his mad secrets.

"By the way, I haven't thanked you for finding the key on Conti and unlocking that vault door," Mark added.

Jessica smiled, nodding. "Anytime. I should thank you for hoisting me up out of that claustrophobic place. If you hadn't, we might still be there."

Mark grinned, feeling awash with warmth for her. He supposed they were lucky, this time. He let the subject drop. "How's the writing coming?" He glanced at her portable computer, set up on a Parsons table that served as her desk.

The work, Jessica thought. *Of course.* She should have known that was why he'd stopped by. With an effort she stifled her disappointment. She'd wanted him to come just to see her. Not to talk about work. "I should be done with all the rough drafts in another two to four weeks.''

''Great.''

''When do you plan to finish the pictures?''

''After I've read your articles. Then I'll know how to approach the subjects.''

So why was he here now? ''Don't tell me.'' She snapped her fingers as inspiration hit. ''You're on another assignment for *Personalities*.''

His smile widened, and he stretched out his legs with appealing languor. ''Yes and no. It's more a personal assignment. I plan to start it up as soon as possible, after we wrap up the series on political wives. There's one hitch.'' He raised his eyes to hers and held her gaze for what seemed an inordinately long time. ''I need a writing partner. Someone who can do the prose, while I snap the prints.''

She held her breath. Her heart was pounding so hard that she feared it would leap out of her chest. Just to be on the safe side, she decided to play it cool. ''Anyone special in mind?'' she asked casually.

His grin widened with the lazy assurance of a man used to getting what he wants. ''Oh yes.''

Her stomach did a flip-flop at the smoldering passion in his eyes. Her movements unhurried, she sank onto the sofa beside him. ''What's the new project about?''

His hand slid over hers, infusing it with warmth. ''It's about small towns and back roads in the United States. I want to know what the appeal is, and I want to see it and understand it through the vision of someone who also cares a lot about life in a small town.''

She felt an ache in her throat, a happiness that made her want to cry. ''Do you have a publisher interested in this, or are you doing it on spec?" she asked, keeping her voice steady with difficulty.

His hand tightened possessively over hers. "It's on spec. My time, my pace. It could take...oh, months before I'd finish."

"And then what?"

"Then I guess it will be up to my partner." He lifted her hand to his lips and kissed it gently. "So what do you think? You know anyone who might be interested? Anyone who wouldn't be afraid to take the risk?"

She knew someone who wanted to marry him. "What about the agency?"

"Noah assures me they can live without me for a couple months. Longer, if they have to. I'm valuable, but I can be useful in innumerable ways." He paused, his eyes serious. "My work is dangerous. I won't sugarcoat that for you."

And she wouldn't deny her feelings. "Living is dangerous. So is loving."

His glance darkened affectionately. "But you do love?" he asked huskily.

Tears of happiness welled up behind her eyes. "Oh, yes, very much."

"Going to tell me who the lucky fellow is?"

"You're the snoop," she said, already unbuttoning his shirt and pressing a kiss to the hollow of his throat. "You guess."

He groaned. The next thing she knew, she was lying prone on the couch, Mark stretched out beside her. He framed her face with his hands. "I don't have to guess," he murmured. "I know. And I love you, too, Jessica Lowell." He kissed her deeply. "Mind you, I'm not promising I'll ever be able to settle down in one place."

"It won't be necessary. As long as I'm with you, I'll have everything I need." Other details were expendable. It was only Mark that mattered. If they could be together, anything else was possible.

"Does this mean you've accepted my offer and agreed to be my partner? Not just temporarily now, like before, but forever and ever." His eyes darkened even more. "As in marriage."

For a second she was too choked up to speak. Finally she managed to compose herself, and when she did, she couldn't resist teasing him as he had teased her. "You drive a hard bargain, Gallagher, but what the heck, I'll pick up the gauntlet. You've got yourself a volunteer— and a life partner."

"For richer, for poorer?"

"In sickness and in health. In danger and out of it." She laughed.

"I'll kiss to that," he murmured happily. And they did.

Harlequin Superromance

CALLOWAY CORNERS

Created by four outstanding Superromance authors, bonded by lifelong friendship and a love of their home state: Sandra Canfield, Tracy Hughes, Katherine Burton and Penny Richards.

CALLOWAY CORNERS

Home of four sisters as different as the seasons, as elusive as the elements; an undiscovered part of Louisiana where time stands still and passion lasts forever.

CALLOWAY CORNERS

Birthplace of the unforgettable Calloway women: *Mariah*, free as the wind, and untamed until she meets the preacher who claims her, body and soul; *Jo*, the fiery, feisty defender of lost causes who loses her heart to a rock and roll man; *Tess*, gentle as a placid lake but tormented by her longing for the town's bad boy and *Eden*, the earth mother who's been so busy giving love she doesn't know how much she needs it until she's awakened by a drifter's kiss . . .

CALLOWAY CORNERS

Coming from Superromance, in 1989:
Mariah, by Sandra Canfield, a January release
Jo, by Tracy Hughes, a February release
Tess, by Katherine Burton, a March release
Eden, by Penny Richards, an April release

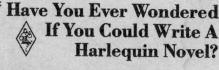

Have You Ever Wondered If You Could Write A Harlequin Novel?

Here's great news—Harlequin is offering a series of cassette tapes to help you do just that. Written by Harlequin editors, these tapes give practical advice on how to make your characters—and your story—come alive. There's a tape for each contemporary romance series Harlequin publishes.

Mail order only

All sales final

TO: **Harlequin Reader Service**
Audiocassette Tape Offer
P.O. Box 1396
Buffalo, NY 14269-1396

I enclose a check/money order payable to HARLEQUIN READER SERVICE® for $9.70 ($8.95 plus 75¢ postage and handling) for EACH tape ordered for the total sum of $_____*
Please send:

☐ Romance and Presents ☐ Intrigue
☐ American Romance ☐ Temptation
☐ Superromance ☐ All five tapes ($38.80 total)

Signature_____
(please print clearly)
Name:_____
Address:_____
State:_____ Zip:_____

*Iowa and New York residents add appropriate sales tax.

AUDIO-H

Harlequin Temptation dares to be different!

Once in a while, we Temptation editors spot a romance that's truly innovative. To make sure *you* don't miss any one of these outstanding selections, we'll mark them for you.

EDITOR'S CHOICE

When the "Editors' Choice" fold-back appears on a Temptation cover, you'll know we've found that extra-special page-turner!

THE *Temptation* EDITORS